A FEW MEN FAITHFUL

A KAVANAGH STORY

JIM WILLS

Carswell House Books

Cover Design: Wade Nelligan

ISBN: 1448685575; EAN-13: 9781448685578

Printed by Book Surge for Create Space.

For

Mary G. Wills,

Survivor to the End,

Gratia Plena.

BEGINNINGS

A Few Men Faithful is the inevitable start of the Kavanagh stories, where the founding images appear, the sides chosen, the events occur and the treacheries begin that drive these men through the generations. From Crossmaglen to Melbourne, Dublin to New York, memories are long among the Irish. Inaccurate, perhaps, prejudiced, perhaps, but they remain decidedly long, distinctly Irish. Kinsale, the Boyne, the Great Hunger, *Cúchulainn*, Penal Laws, Cromwell, Wolfe Tone, Finn McCool, Pius IX, Parnell, Easter Rising, Civil War, Bloody Sundays, the Troubles, live in a kind of historical holy land where all are one in time, memory, myth, grievance, keening, anger, retribution, atonement.

For a crucial period, this was particularly true in the United States. It is well known that many thousands reached North America in the mid-nineteenth century, flock upon flock of ragged, starving birds caged in coffin ships. It is less well known precisely why they had no choice but to leave and what heavy baggage they brought with them. For the exiles, the agonies of *An Gorta Mór* (The Great Hunger)—the starvation amid plenty that began in stark earnest during 1845—melded in nightmare with the splash of bodies dumped overboard to feed the grinning maw of diaspora. In reality and retelling, the mouths of skeletal corpses stuffed with grass they could not swallow, dead and living stacked together like cord wood in relief house beds, a priest's report of cannibalism, contrasted grimly with the round bellies of clean sails and holds full of Irish grain, bacon, butter, beef, headed for England during those same years.

These memories could have been borne, perhaps, but the deep wound of being staked out as part of Empire yet allowed to starve unaided did not heal and stayed fresh in exile through the decades. In 1841, the population of the island was roughly estimated at 8.5 million; by 1851 it was 6.5 million: more than a million died, perhaps two, if it were possible to count the peasants buried without ceremony where they dropped of hunger or disease, the rest scattered on the wind or slipped beneath the waves. Abroad, hate hardened to adamantine, despite some spluttering political changes at home. Here is the source, not of North America's happy Paddy or the so-called luck of the Irish, but of that most Irish of characteristics—rage—deep, abiding, inextinguishable, genetic. The anger of centuries and the memory of the *Gael* is not a placid combination, despite the gallows humor, the graveyard wit.

With a disturbingly modern ring, Michael Davitt, founder of the Irish Land League, used the word "holocaust" in 1904 to describe *An Gorta Mór*. In *The Irish Sketch-Book*, the English novelist William Makepeace Thackeray anticipated him in 1843 and characterized the centuries long occupation of Ireland as:

> ... a frightful document against ourselves...one of the most melancholy stories in the whole world of insolence, rapine, brutal, endless slaughter and persecution on the part of the English master. There is no crime ever invented by eastern or western barbarians, no torture or Roman persecution or Spanish inquisition, no tyranny of Nero or Alva, but can be matched in the history of England in Ireland.

A known author, though not yet famous, Thackeray was politically astute enough to write this two volume diary of his Irish travels under the pseudonym M. A. Titmarsh.

Earlier yet, well before the Great Hunger began but in the shadow of the savagely repressed 1798 Irish Rebellion, Sydney Smith, the English wit, clergyman and raconteur, observed in his *Letters to Peter Plymley* (1807-1808): "The moment the very name of Ireland is mentioned, the English seem to bid adieu to common feeling, common prudence, and common sense, and to act with the barbarity of tyrants, and the fatuity of idiots." His regret and outrage were quite evident: "Our conduct to Ireland ... has been that of a man who subscribes to hospitals, weeps at charity sermons, carries out broth and blankets to beggars, and then comes home and beats his wife and children." Smith well understood the inevitable consequences:

> I detest that state of society which extends unequal degrees of protection to different creeds and persuasions; and I cannot describe to you the contempt I feel for a man who, calling himself a statesman, defends a system which fills the heart of every Irishman with treason, and makes his allegiance prudence, not choice.

These accounts, eyewitness and contemporary though they are, may or may not be completely accurate or wholly objective, especially in the face of today's revisionist, apologist historians. Nevertheless, for decades the Irish in the United States husbanded the images, nursed the anger, and ignored the demonizing of what was to become the IRA. People like the Fenian John Devoy and the Tammany powerhouse Judge Daniel Cohalan in Manhattan, Joe McGarrity in Philadelphia, tended the revolutionary forge during the dark years between 1867 and 1916. Through the *Clann na Gael*, they kept the hate alive when Ireland itself seemed content, or at least resolved, to patiently continue a possession, never a nation. McGarrity, in particular, was of enormous influence in the US and Ireland. His name was used to sign IRA communiqués long after his death and well into the 1960s; yet another name invoked from the historical holy land.

Devoy and Cohalan disagreed vehemently with Eamon de Valera during his fund-raising trip to the United States in 1919. Fresh from Lincoln Prison in England, and well away from the fighting at home, already de Valera was developing into the verbose, self-centered, uncertain, mystifying politician he was to become in much later years. Both Cohalan and Devoy, on the other hand, continued for a time as the radical advocates of nationhood for Ireland by force of arms, no compromise, no accommodation, no partition. The devastating splits in Ireland and the United States came shortly afterwards. For some, de Valera became a hero; for some a traitor; so, too, Michael Collins.

The doomed Easter Rising of 1916, where *A Few Men Faithful* begins, eventually did much more than merely solidify a very real, urgent, widespread sense of Irish nationalism for the first time. It winnowed the barren seeds of the Irish Civil War—that hidden, mildewed furrow in the psyche of the *Gael* whose rotting smell continues to this day. That deeply divisive, merciless internecine war, scarcely mentioned, barely chronicled, wrote yet more hagiographies of martyred Irish saints and sent out other waves of blooded exiles, like Danny Kavanagh of this story. Most importantly, the Easter Rising taught politicians and revolutionaries alike a crucial lesson. The French failed to send arms and troops to Wolf Tone and the United Irishmen in 1798. The Germans failed to send arms, ammunition, and Irish POWs to Sir Roger Casement and the Irish Volunteers in 1916. Thereafter, Irish Republicans at home turned their faces from Europe and looked west, to the United States, where men like Devoy, Cohalan, McGarrity, and, later, George Harrison, fed the nationalist forge by stoking it with guns and money.

They could not have done it, nor could they continue to do it, without believers of long memory, glittering diamond hard anger. These are the men and women who, for more than eighty years, raised the funds, shipped the arms and kept the true faith: a united thirty-two county Ireland, a nation without partition, without ties to a past they repudiate as told by storytellers other than themselves. That the Irish Republic no longer seems interested means nothing.

The key figures in the first three Kavanagh stories: Danny, born in Crossmaglen, South Armagh, 1896; Jack, born in Philadelphia, Pennsylvania, 1942; Chris, born in Milltown, North Armagh, 2000, are such men. Their lives are complex, their beliefs conflicting, their anger constant, their souls hammered and rifled like gun barrels. From the 19th to the 21st century, one thing unites them beyond the name, the images, the legacy, the fury. Each displays the stigmata of the *Gael*: to bleed always, never healing. If this is the luck of the Irish, all three have it most completely. If this is the curse of the Irish, each exorcises his demons in his own way.

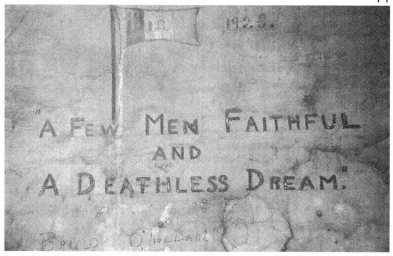

In 1923, Brigid O'Mullane, an anti-Treaty Republican prisoner jailed by her Pro-Treaty, Free-State former comrades in arms, inscribed these words on the wall of a damp and tiny cell in Kilmainham Gaol on Inchicore Road in Dublin: "A Few Men Faithful and a Deathless Dream." Above the inscription is a painting of the Irish Tricolor. Though badly faded by damp and time, it remains an exceptionally powerful icon for men like the Kavanaghs, just like the austere killing wall in the Stonebreakers yard of the Kilmainham shown the front cover of this book. They live that deathless dream with agonizing faithfulness; they are the few, the terrible beauty born that will not die.

In *Philly MC*, the second of the Kavanagh stories, the redoubtable, whimsical beatnik Hose Ramirez tells young Jack Kavanagh that becoming a professional baseball player is "a long, slow road for all but the best." Writing fiction is like that, too; perhaps more so. Without supporters, team-mates, during the uncertain years of wandering in the bush-league wilderness, perseverance and belief are nearly impossible.

Thank you, Beth and Jerry Bentley, for your generous support and ceaseless faith. Thank you, Wendy Carlson, for coming into my life.

JTW, December, 2009

Now days are dragon-ridden, the nightmare

Rides upon sleep.....‡

‡W.B. Yeats, "Nineteen Hundred and Nineteen."

CHAPTERS

PART I

ECHO OF THE THOMPSON GUN

1. "WHEREVER GREEN IS WORN"

The three young brothers sat together, backs against a low stone wall, listening to the muzzles cracking and the bullets hissing over their heads. Casually, they competed to see who could identify the heavier arms being fired at them. "Vickers, that's sure." "No, no, ye daft twit, it's one a them new Lewis guns. Where's yer ears, man, in yer pants?" On the outside, they seemed unconcerned, almost nonchalant, joking and laughing, before, in turn, they knelt to fire over the wall at the Tommies. Danny, the youngest, calmly puffed his pipe, regarded the trembling air with satisfaction and sniffed the cordite with relish. On the inside, they all felt the exhilaration of revenge, gloried in being on the side of right, yearned for the deathless Republican dream. None had ever killed a man. Many on the barricades opposite had.

Jack Kavanagh, the eldest, turned to Mick, next in age. "What's your thought? Will we whip the bastards this time?" He said it with a rhetorical smile. As usual, the taciturn middle brother said nothing; waiting for the answer he knew was coming from Danny, the most talkative of the three. Danny pulled the pipe from his mouth, spat reflectively, and said: "'Soon or Never,' as the saying goes. At least we can collect on a few markers." The other two nodded, their lips hardening to thin lines. Once the artillery started on them, they knew they were finished. But all three understood it had to be done.

They watched with mild amusement as one of their officers slithered toward them on his belly. "Danny, you and the brothers get out front and cover us while we do it. Dev's idea." The order was shouted over the new and very near rattle of a British Vickers heavy machine gun that was quickly overwhelmed by the incoming whistle and explosion of an eighteen pounder field gun shell. Dust and pieces of brick hailed down on their slouch hats. "Right, Captain, we're for it." Danny Kavanagh and his brothers slung their old Mausers over their backs and headed for sniping positions outside the trenches and barricades around Boland's Flour Mill in Dublin. The shelling, the massed machine gun and rifle fire, made the position of the 3rd Brigade of the Irish Volunteers untenable. Everyone knew that. Everyone knew, too, that their Brigade Commander, Eamon de Valera, was a mathematics teacher, no military man and very near to breaking point.

Captain Cullen responded to de Valera's diversion scheme with alacrity, naïve bravado; so had three of his men. They crouched behind the stone wall that overlooked the Grand Canal Basin and watched the Kavanaghs spread out in front of them. They all hoped Dev's plan worked, even for a while, to take the pressure off. It was late Tuesday afternoon, April 25, 1916, and British reinforcements had arrived, along with their field guns. Except for the officers, most of the rank and file among the enemy were Irish, too, men who traded the King's shilling for French trenches.

The three Kavanaghs were in the minority among the Irish Volunteers that Easter week: north country men from County Armagh, familiar with weapons from boyhood, more than ready for a fight, members of the militant and very secret Irish Republican Brotherhood. Weathered, muscular, tough. Their coloring was a Celtic essay: Jack, black haired, brown eyed, the tallest; Mick, red haired, pale, blue eyed; and the auburn haired Danny of the green, green eyes. Jack continued the head of the family tradition as a small farmer of small success in Crossmaglen, where they all were born. Mick, the mechanic, could not help his fascination with the new tractors and motor cars. Danny, the journeyman carpenter, had more knowledge of wood than the trees. Poaching and smuggling through the Gap of Armagh, generations old vocations, took up the rest of their time.

Work hardened, practical, men of their hands, they were not among the Dublin intellectuals, the dreamers, like the contemplative poet, Padraig Pearse, who believed myth must triumph over history, right over steel, rhetoric over legislation. In Ireland, both Catholics and Protestants who thought as he did had been making magnificent rebellious plans, delaying them interminably, then sliding into the greasy clay pit of political infighting and treachery for time out of mind. The speeches were grand, no doubt, but the link among them was failure and minor poetry.

Witty, somewhere between skeptical and hostile about religion, fond of a drink, a song, the girls, at bottom the Kavanaghs were grim, determined men, survivors of Pearse's rhetorical flourish of the "Fenian dead," inheritors of famine haunt and flogging scream. Their purpose was straight-forward, six hundred years old, hard as the stones in the Armagh fields: drive the English invader into the Irish Sea—forever—no matter the cost or the wait. It was their core belief; not reasoned, passed through the umbilical cord.

They had little time for and less understanding of the Citizen Army, the city-bred fledgling socialist workers who followed James Connolly and Jim Larkin under the Starry Plough flag. To the Kavanaghs, a workers' state had no meaning. They, and country IRB men like them, wanted all the land back, the landlords gone, the crushing rents a mere sour memory, and, most of all, revenge that was physical, not political. In 1916, they still lived the horror years of the Famine Queen, more than seventy years after their great grandparents were evicted from their holding and starved in a ditch while Queen Victoria drank Scotch and roasted potatoes at Balmoral. Dublin that Easter week retold the old story of Ireland: splits in the ranks, rancorous division upon division over politics, spies upon spies, Irishmen facing Irishmen over rifle barrels, self-directed inner rage turned to killing.

Stationed twenty yards apart, the brothers watched as the four men advanced toward the old, empty stone tower two hundred yards in front of their position. Cover was not good; progress slow. Lee-Enfield rounds whipped by them, kicking up clouds of rank coal dust, chipping off brick. Modern, accurate, trenches tested, every one of the rebels longed for a Lee-Enfield rifle.

Just turned twenty, unmarried, Danny Kavanagh was definitely the best shot. In Crossmaglen, he was an occasional poacher of legendary success, bringing home the Christmas deer slung over his shoulders. He lined up the helmet of a British soldier in his iron sights and gently squeezed off a round. Even at 100 yards, the clank of metal being pierced could be heard above the noise of battle. He blinked hard, his teeth crushing the stem of his stubby pipe. The remaining enemy helmets popped out of sight like mushrooms sucked back into the ground.

Captain Cullen and his men still had fifty yards to go. They made a strange squad: none in uniform, all in lapelled jackets, collars, ties, soft hats. Shabby, but disciplined. One, Pat Brennan, a butcher from Dublin's Moore Street, tried to advance from a pile of paving stones to an overturned wagon with its dead and bloated horse. He collapsed in a heap, shot through the body, legs kicking briefly at the horse's taut stomach. Jack Kavanagh leaped from his position, cleared the rubble in a bound and made for them at a crouching run. Hearts in their dry mouths, Danny and Mick covered him until he was safe among them. Of the three, Jack was the bravest, the most reckless, easily the most angry.

The last hundred feet were the worst. Danny and Mick fired as rapidly as they could, hoping to appear many rather than two. The barrels of their ancient German Mausers began to overheat. They were leftovers from the arms shipment paid for by Joe McGarrity from Philadelphia and landed at Howth by Erskine Childers in 1914. On their stomachs, the detail of Irish Volunteers finally made it into the base of the tower. Enemy fire resumed in the direction of Boland's Mill for the time. From his position, Danny could see Captain Cullen emerge on top of the tower; smoke from the burning buildings obscuring him from the enemy for as long as he needed. Cullen knelt, tied the green flag to a pike and hoisted it. The afternoon was close, dull, cloudy, and the fires had created a fitful, swirling wind around the tower. The flag hung limp for a second, then tried to unfurl. It might have been the famous bedspread of the Countess Markievicz. It wasn't; no one seemed to know where it came from, but it was emblazoned with the outrageous treason: "Irish Republic."

An odd, muted cheer, almost a moan of desperation, could be heard faintly from the Irish lines. Danny Kavanagh crouched transfixed, looking over the sights of his Mauser.

Time slowed and stopped in a diamond moment of his life, soul deep, never to be forgotten, added to the ulcerous hate passed through the generations. The flag furling, the volunteers emerging from the base of the tower. His oldest brother, Jack, leaving his feet and flipping onto his back as if slapped by the hand of an invisible angry god. Shot through the head, dead in a second. His slouch hat seemed to take minutes to sail to the ground. From that instant, young Danny Kavanagh was changed utterly. He could see Jack's wife and children, smiling in the tiny garden, at home in Crossmaglen. The abiding fury created by that image would never leave him till the day he died.

Mick tried, but he knew he could not stop him. Danny ran upright, in full view, to his brother's body, bullets ripping past him, shredding his jacket. Cullen and his men watched him come, mouths open, more in disbelief than fear for his life. It was as if he ran surrounded by a bubble of safety, impenetrable. One look at Jack's mangled head, and the blinding Kavanagh anger took him. Long German bayonet fixed, Danny charged the British position. One, perhaps two, maybe three soldiers who had survived the Hun in Flanders went down in Dublin internecine squalor. Then Mick

Kavanagh could see the rifle butt poised over his brother; it came down again and again. The body was pushed over the English barricade, rolled onto its face and lay still.

Perhaps the price was worth the effect. The enemy turned their attention and their field gun on the old tower, rather than the mill. The inevitable was forestalled. The green bedspread continued to fly.

Night came damp, moonless, cheerless among the Irish Volunteers at Boland's Mill. De Valera's command was isolated across the River Liffey, east of the city center. Pearse and Plunkett and their people had taken the central General Post Office on Sackville Street, but all their early success got them was more attention from the enemy than the other positions in the city. The *Aud*, the arms ship from Germany, had not arrived to supply the entire country; Sir Roger Casement had been caught; no Irish prisoners of war, freed by the Germans, marched in to die alongside them; a mere $1000 had arrived from Joe McGarrity in Philadelphia, along with a few Thompson submachine guns. The fighting outside Dublin was sporadic, desultory, mostly it had been called off, once Eoin MacNeill countermanded the orders for a rebellion from the more militant commanders of the Irish Volunteers.

An Easter Rising was yet another grand gesture, no doubt, borne of longing, principle, belief, reprisal, but it would fail as the others had failed: 1798, 1843, 1867. They knew it would, just as well as they knew it was necessary for several key reasons. In 1886, Parnell, the uncrowned king of Ireland, lost the real battle in London for Irish Home Rule, then his life. Later, John Redmond agreed to the exclusion of Ulster from a version of it—temporarily it was said—until after the war in Europe, it was said. In 1913, Edward Carson and James Craig publicly armed the paramilitary, anti-Home-Rule Loyalist Volunteer Force in Ulster—ironically with German weapons— with the full and mutinous support of the British garrison at the Curragh. The Irish Volunteers, organized in response a year later, were definitely not allowed to bear arms. Over the decades and blood since its foundation in 1858, the Irish Republican Brotherhood expression now had become a secret refrain sighing on the Atlantic wind; much, much more than a political saw or seditious proverb: "Soon or Never;" soon they must win or they never would.

In the chill damp, Mick Kavanagh slithered forward and retrieved the body of his oldest brother. Reverently, he emptied his pockets of the few possessions Jack's wife would want, straightened his tie and arranged his jacket, before folding the hands over the chest. As the next son in age, he slipped his father's brass pocket watch into his pocket. For the wife's sake, he regretted there were no priests among them for the last rites. The priests would not come until much later, and the more radical among the Irish Republican Brotherhood contingent in the Irish Volunteers did not want them, a refusal hardened by the fact that Pius IX had excommunicated all the Fenians in 1869, including Jimmy, the father of the Kavanagh boys.

Something of sedition scholar, Jimmy would kick off his muck covered boots in front of the turf fire at home in Crossmaglen and once more say to his sons over his jar: "Ah, we've not done well with the Popes now have we boys? Priests neither. Think of old Adrian IV who told that English bastard Henry II to conquer Ireland in 1155. Then consider the power hungry arsewipe, Alexander VIII, who ordered the *Te Deum* sung across Europe when his bum boy, King Billy, won the Battle of the Boyne in 1690. Then Pius VII supported the English veto in 1816. Old Pius IX was just following their lead when he excommunicated the lot of us. I'm in fine company. I'll not have to remind you about the Irish hierarchy in 1863 or Dublin's Archbishop Cullen in 1865. We'll leave Cromwell out of it for the time." These were the articles of faith, the apostles' creed, for the Kavanagh men. Only the Kavanagh women kept the rosaries polished for the keening. The men went to church when they must—to keep the peace—but theirs was another religion.

Lying on his face, blowing dark, sticky bubbles in his own blood, Danny Kavanagh was neither conscious nor unconscious. In a swoon of images, the memory broke on him like stepping through a low doorway, light to dark. It was textured, living, real, the color, sound, the perfume of burning turf, the oil lamp's yellow, pulsing bloom on shadowed whitewash. His mother sat at the wooden table in the kitchen, head in her hands, puzzling over the official letter between her red elbows propped on the scrubbed top. Her first language was Gaelic, and written English came slowly to her. Then the rocking and moaning started. In May, 1906, Jimmy Kavanagh was executed by firing squad in the Stonebreakers Yard of Kilmainham Gaol in Dublin. They finally caught up with him for his part in the dynamite plots in England during the winter of 1883-84. The charges were sedition and murder—and belonging to the Irish Republican Brotherhood that everyone in Ireland thought had ceased to exist. Dublin Castle did not feel it necessary to ship the body home to County Armagh. The corpse was thrown into a pit on Arbour Hill, then covered with quicklime. The hill had plenty of space left for more pits, more martyrs dissolving in lime.

Mick knew that retrieving Danny would be much, much more difficult. It took an hour to reach him. He expected dead weight, but as he lay side by side with his brother, directly beneath the English barricade, Mick could hear the foaming, ragged breathing of the living as he smelled the pipe smoke and tea of the enemy.

"Can you speak, Danny?" The battered head turned a slow negative, mouth full of clotting blood. "Can you move, man?" The smashed face nodded a slow affirmative. Danny Kavanagh spit out the blood and mumbled "crazy fucker" to his only brother. As they crawled the hundreds of yards back to the rebel lines, Danny seemed to be losing more blood than humanly possible, a dark slug smear marking their path.

"That was the most courageous or foolhardy thing I've ever seen, Mick. Your brother lives up to the Armagh reputation for the savage, the madman and the dead shot. But, and I'm sorry to say it, he'll die by morning unless we can get him to Jim Ryan at the GPO. He's the only one with any sort of combat wound experience. I'm a doctor as well, but I've no knowledge of this extent of trauma, no equipment, no medicines left."

"Thanks for your concern, Dr. Kelly, but I'm thinking it'll be a difficult bit of ground to travel between here and there, just now."

"So it would, but it seems that someone managed to commandeer a British motorbike that might just need a driver to take messages to Pearse at the GPO. Passengers definitely permitted. Are you game, man?"

"Indeed I am, sir. I've only driven one a few times, not far. Usually, I just fixed their tires and such at the garage, but it's not that difficult. After all, it's really a bicycle with a motor." He spoke with the offhand confidence of youth, not any real experience. The sight of his dead brother did not leave the front of his mind.

"For Danny's sake, I hope you're right, so I do."

The motorcycle was a Triumph Model H, the "Trusty Triumph" used by Allied dispatch riders in France. Except for the military and the police, they were uncommon in Ireland then; toys for landowners' sons, transport for the detested Royal Irish Constabulary. Unfortunately, or fortunately, this one had a sidecar: fortunate for the injured passenger, unfortunate for the fledgling driver, because it made the machine much more difficult to control. Leaning in the wrong direction when rounding a corner could flip the rig in an instant, ejecting the passenger into the night, like a sack of coal. Mick tried to remember the controls near the fire the Volunteers made to brew their tea. He found the throttle, the spark advance, the kick starter, brake, clutch. Perhaps it could be done. Perhaps—with luck.

"Where's the man Kavanagh? I need to speak with him now." Like most of the commanders during Easter week, Eamon de Valera was an intellectual. He might not have been much of a military man, but he was imperious and used to being obeyed immediately. Unusually tall, dark, thin, bespectacled, his somber, sagging face was couched in sadness by a thick moustache. Ordinarily, he looked on the verge of tears. Now, worry, lack of sleep, fear, gave his lanky frame the tension of a long German bayonet. His red rimmed eyes glowed in a disconcerting, blank stare that flicked from object to object. Unlike most of the Irish Volunteers, Dev wore full uniform, making him look rather foreign. Perhaps the feeling originated from his dead Spanish father or the Irish mother who, some said, abandoned him, or the fact he was born in New York City and retained his American citizenship. Despite his imperious manner, de Valera commanded immense respect and loyalty from the men under his command at Boland's Mill.

Captain Cullen pointed Mick out by the fire. De Valera strode over, towering above all around him. The firelight accentuated the dark bags under his averted eyes, the morose skin of his face. "Right, Kavanagh, I was sorry to hear of your one brother killed and the other wounded. Ireland will remember them both when we drive the British from our land and establish our right to a nation. For their sake, for our sake, for the sake of history, you must make it to the GPO and give these messages to Padraig Pearse. The whole course of the rising depends on it." Mick stood rigid, still, assaulted by the images of the afternoon. The muscles worked in his jaw. De Valera shook Mick's hand quickly, turned on his heel and stalked away, like some dreaming, tormented stork.

Dev was never one to miss an opportunity for a speech. It was clear from the first word that he was talking for the benefit of his men. Not one among them thought there was any chance. They were out manned, overwhelmed by modern weaponry. Worse, the people of Dublin were against them. Those citizens of the United Kingdom of Great Britain and Ireland were much more concerned in 1916 with putting bread on the table. That was the city, among the prosperous. In the agricultural countryside, bread was a luxury, because most of the grain to make it went as rent to England, along with the bacon, butter, beef. Potatoes remained the usual and only fare, if the blight didn't come again. In the steaming heap and vermin playground of the Dublin slums, there was no fare at all.

From his post behind the pile of ledger books, coal sacks, chairs, typewriters stacked in front of the Georgian Sackville Street entrance to the General Post Office, Sean Hurley could see British troops attempting to barricade the street. They were careful but hardly impervious to the Irish marksmen in the windows around them, even though the wide, dark street was lit only by fires. "It's just a matter of time," he thought with a small smile. Next to him stood his cousin, Michael Collins, the "Big Fella," who would live to become the most dangerous, most enigmatic man in Ireland. Collins, ADC to the Director of Operations, Joseph Mary Plunkett, with the rank of Staff Captain, was one of the few in the Post Office wearing the resplendent green uniform of the Irish Volunteers. The closest of friends since boyhood, Hurley and Collins spoke little, knowing each other's thoughts, wordlessly sharing their bright dream of an Irish nation, no matter the cost. Like the Kavanaghs from South Armagh, they hoped the wait was nearly over. "Soon or Never" once more.

"Jaysus Murphy, Michael, will you just look at that." Around the partially finished barricade, through the fire smoke from Sackville Street, a military motorcycle suddenly appeared, close, apparently from nowhere. The demented driver had little training, anyone could see that. He was going much too fast, and, despite his attempts to correct it, the single wheel of the sidecar hovered uncertainly, nearly a foot off the ground, then bounced to the cobbles, then rose again. The passenger's face was heavily bandaged in white gauze turned red on one side. Such a bizarre sight momentarily froze the normally unflappable British troops, even their snipers held back, though a few less experienced men stood to gawk before being pulled down by more battle hardened hands. Neither side knew who they were at first, so no one fired. The silence was dead still, hard on ears used to pitched battle, until Mick Kavanagh began screaming, "*Éirinn go bloody Brách*, goddamn it, here I come, lads."

Inside the GPO, the riflemen saw the rider's civilian clothes, heard him shout, so they opened up on the enemy barricade, concentrating on the Vickers gun position that could have cut the motorcycle down in a second.

Mick Kavanagh saw no other way. He swerved sharply left, headed the bike between the massive columns in the middle of the portico and made directly for the broad doorway. At least he had the sense to slow down, but he cracked over the low curbing so fast that he bit his cheek and his kidneys bounded on their moorings. Beside him, Danny bounced in the sidecar like a haunch of dressed beef. As the Triumph hit the doorway, Mick could see the muzzle flashes of rifle and

shotgun rounds headed for the British positions.   He
smashed through the makeshift barrier, spraying typewriters.
Once the tires hit the slick marble of the foyer, made slicker
by melting window glass, the bike skidded 180 degrees,
ending up against a long mahogany counter, pointing in the
direction from which it had come.

The large room was completely silent for long seconds;
eyes white in faces gunpowder black; then a laugh, then a
cheer for the brave, the foolhardy, the Irish. Casually,
Michael Collins strode over to the motorcycle, regarding it as
he would if he were a prospective buyer in a showroom. He
turned on the brilliant, boyish smile and said to Mick, "Well
now, boyo, and that was a dramatic entrance suitable for the
Court Theater. *Deus ex machina*, don'tcha know. You *are*
one of us, I trust?"

"Yes, sir, Mick Kavanagh, South Armagh IRB. Messages
for Pearse from de Valera. Some ride that. These
motorbikes are fantastic. Have a go, sir?"

"Charmed, I'm sure. Unfortunately, I'm a bit tied up at the
moment. Nevertheless, I do have a pressing appointment
with a divine young nurse by the name of Theresa tomorrow.
Perhaps then, if you would be so kind."

"Certainly, sir, I'll be sure to be here."

"Of that I have no doubt."

Collins took a closer look at the inert passenger. Curiosity, then deep concern, spread over his face. "Your man is in a bad way, Kavanagh. Is he alive?"

"My brother, sir. Danny. Tom Kelly said Jim Ryan could patch him back together."

The deep creases in Collins' brow said the brother was past hope. He took off his officer's cap, slowly smoothed the shock of brown hair aside and turned to Sean Hurley: "Right, Sean, get some men and take this man to Doctor Ryan. Give them both a strong shot of whiskey, too, one for his insanity, the other for his life." This was a large concession from Michael Collins. He was sensitive to the historical sneer about the 1798 Irish rebels needing drink for courage, so he had gone so far as to pour two tierces of porter down a drain in front of his astonished men. But this, this was an exception. "The messages, man, give them to me. I'll get them to the Commandant. You attend to your brother. Then you can start using those God awful rifles you brought with you. Bloody Mausers." Collins turned to go. He stopped, briefly, a sour look on his face as he stared at the men on their knees, telling the beads. "And we're supposed to be an army. God help us. What we need is more and better weapons from McGarrity and his lot in the States, not more Hail Marys. Damned sad lot of revolutionaries we are."

2. "Bandoleer of Lead"

Doctor Jim Ryan certainly did not need yet another casualty to look after, but this wound was so interesting that, despite the mayhem surrounding him, his clinical self took over. He hadn't seen such a mess since he served in the British Army during the Boer War, especially when the patient continued breathing. Even Connolly's shattered ankle wasn't nearly this bad. "Ah, yes. Mick, what's the brother's name then?"

"Danny, sir. Will he live?"

"If I had a hospital, nurses, time, luck, yes. Here, I'm just not sure, though your brother's head seems to be made of iron. It's a wonder the eye hasn't been put out, but his skull is fractured, how badly I don't know, and he's lost a lot of blood. I've no morphine left, so I'll have to stitch him up without. If he survives, the scar will mark him for life."

Mick Kavanagh looked down at his brother. Marked for life he certainly would be. The deep smash of the rifle butt's steel plate ran from his hairline, over his left eye, and down to his collapsed cheekbone. Danny Kavanagh had been a handsome young man, tall for a country Irishman, barrel chested, oak strong, the fox among the chickens with the ladies of Crossmaglen and Cullyhanna on market days. The auburn hair, green eyes and fine tenor singing voice helped. Mick Kavanagh thought that, if Danny survived, his effect on women was gone and his usefulness to the IRB was over. Time did not prove him right on either point.

The end became a certainty when the British gunboat *Helga* steamed up the Liffey and began the heavy shelling with her deck guns, looking to blast a clear line of fire to the GPO. The situation deteriorated immediately, the fires rapidly became worse and the General Post Office was almost completely surrounded by Thursday, April 27, 1916. The rebels stuck close to the walls on the upper floors to avoid collapsing the fire weakened joists. Even the intellectual commanders began to think that evacuation or surrender had become matters, not of courage, but humanity.

Attempt after attempt was made to escape the inferno and the British guns by tunneling through shop walls, then making a dash through the raking crossfire that swept Moore Street. Nothing worked. To fight on meant the entire rebel leadership would die, just as many Dublin civilians already had. The call for a cease fire had to come from Padraig Pearse. It had not been issued yet, because he hadn't finished it yet. His adjutant, Winnie Carney, typed and retyped it, kneeling behind a post office counter. The survivors waited.

One of them, Michael Collins, the "Big Fella," was feeling decidedly small after seeing his boyhood friend, Sean Hurley, cut down in one attempt to breach the British encirclement. Against his own orders, he had secured a bottle of Jameson Irish Whiskey. It dangled from one hand; the other held a new Thompson submachine gun from America, useless now, without ammunition. Collins wandered the ground floor of the GPO in a dream of death, sleeplessness, noise and smoke.

"Excuse me, sir, but the brother here certainly could use a drink." Mick Kavanagh was never one to hold back when a bottle of the Irish showed nearby, especially that smooth variety distilled nearby on the banks of the Liffey.

"Ah, and so it is. Kavanagh, isn't it?"

"Right, sir, Mick. And here's the brother, Danny, almost good as new, thanks to Doctor Ryan."

Staring at Danny's heavily bandaged head, Collins handed Mick the bottle. He took a long pull and passed it to Danny, who did the same, then returned it to Collins.

"You live a charmed life, Kavanagh. Not one man in ten thought you'd live to see the sun another day when you came here. You must have an Irish saint in your family."

Danny's voice was thick, muzzled, from damage, fatigue, pain, loss of blood. "No saints. Fenians, banshees. Better company."

"Kavanagh, that's the most honorable thing I've heard these last two days. 'Long life to you, a wet mouth, and death in Ireland.'" Collins raised the bottle in a toast to this impossible survivor.

Mick the mechanic couldn't help but admire the weapon: "That's a fine new gun you've got there, sir. Never seen one before. How goes it out there?"

"Don't you have eyes and ears, man? We're surrounded, cut off, running out of ammunition, supplies, water. Joe McGarrity sent us a few of these splendid weapons from Philadelphia, USA. They're very new, very effective, but what good are they without shells? Bloody shambles. No planning. There's no sense in all of us being blasted into the ground when we can't fight back from such a fixed position. I'm certain that Mr. Pearse will be calling a cease fire soon, once he composes the proper document, naturally." The brothers could not tell if he was being sincere or sarcastic with this last remark. He seemed drained, his jaunty spirit extinguished for the moment, the gray eyes shrouded, glazed.

"Any chance of evacuation, sir?"

"No, we've tried several times, as you well know. The bastards have us trapped, but we'll try to establish a new HQ tomorrow. However, you Kavanaghs have fought as well and much as any man here alive, and, besides, you're IRB. If you feel you can make a break, I'd do it now. That motorbike you came in on is still where you left it. Your choice, gentlemen, your choice. It's difficult to know how the British will be treating us when we give in, anyway. Here, have another, before I go."

Collins watched them, considering, planning meticulously for the future, as always. The spirit returned, eyes steel hard. "Tell you what, boys. There might be some resistance to you two trying for it on your own, but if I tell the Commandant I have a mission for you, things will go a lot easier. Are you with me?"

Mick looked to his brother, and Danny shrugged. Not positive, not negative.

"Right, then. Here's the idea. If you make it, head for Dundalk. There's a wee lad up there who goes by the name of Big Matt O'Faolain, from Mayo originally. He's one of ours—IRB—not Citizen Army, thank Christ. He and his lads were ready for the fight, but I think they probably all disappeared into the hedgerows when the *Aud* didn't land the guns and the *Clann na Gael* in America didn't come through as planned. You two find him and tell him exactly, precisely what happened here and that I'll be contacting him shortly to reorganize. We have much work left to do. After this bloody mess sorts itself out. No matter what happens, I won't forget you two eejits. We need a lot more of your sort. Let me know what you decide."

Collins had gone, and the two brothers were left by themselves. "Well, Danny old son, what's your fancy? Do we go for Collins' plan and maybe get killed, or stay here and end up in a cell in England, or lined up against a wall in the Kilmainham and shot for our trouble? My thought is we should stick in here with the lads. Our da wouldn't have us run from the Brits."

"No Arbour Hill yet, Mick. Jack's family to think of—and your own. Some of us have to live to fight. Talk to Collins."

Even when there were three of them, Danny's judgment usually went for gospel. He might have been the youngest, but he had the quickest mind and with the brash bravado of youth thought of himself as the toughest, the most unforgiving.

"Right, Danny boy, don't dander off while I'm gone."

"Not likely."

Every rebel who could still fight wanted them to make it, willed them to make it. There was a certain amount of envy, especially when Padraig Pearse agreed with Michael Collins that they should be allowed the attempt to join up with O'Faolain. For his part, Collins had his own reasons for choosing them among many.

Clearly, Sackville Street was impossible. The barricade was impregnable by now. Moore Street would be riding into a shredding machine. Besides, the English had to know they had tunneled through shop after shop to get there. Perhaps a more direct, less expected route would be better.

"Right, lads, the first bit might be tricky, but there yez are. Best we can do." The speaker was a Dublin man born and bred, Frank Boyle. "It'd be death on foot, but maybe yez can make it through those gobshites on this contraption. Godspeed, so. Don't forget, once you hit the cobbles, turn left for all you're worth; otherwise you'll run smack into the Brit Vickers on Earl. Go right at the first wee lane after Moore. It's narrow, but if you keep yer wits about ye, ye can make it all the way to Dorset without being seen. Just keep to the alleyways near the market. Don't stop for nothing. Now, don't piss yerselfs. Wait for the signal."

Mick and Danny Kavanagh sat on the running motorcycle in front of the tall double doors that opened onto Henry Street; Mick hunched over the bars, Danny huddled in the sidecar, two sand bags under his feet to keep the third wheel on the road. The Volunteers Michael Collins assigned to the job were near, waiting. Frank Boyle stood closest. Suddenly, there was a fusillade from the rebels on the Sackville Street side, and Mick felt Boyle's hand slap him hard on the shoulder, just as the doors swung open.

Danny Kavanagh couldn't manage a yell, but he tried anyway. As they started, he called out. "*Éirinn go* fuckin *Brách*, lads. See you in Armagh." No one heard him, even the driver of the trusty Triumph.

The first mistake happened quickly. Just outside the door stood an iron hitching post. All Mick could see was a squat dark mass, backlit by fire. He tried to swerve but not enough; the sidecar smashed directly into it. "Gobshite," from Danny, "you've broke it." Even if he had heard him, Mick was too busy to answer. He pushed the bike away from the post with his foot and sped down Henry Street, just as a Lewis gun opened up from 200 yards away, too far for accuracy.

Hardly a surprise start. The rods that held the sidecar to the frame had bent at a crazy angle. The British snipers were good and marked them quickly. The fires lit the street fairly well but with wide gaps of dark, and smears of dense black smoke from the nearby oil works snaked through the orange glare like greasy banners. They lined up on the Shinner bastards trying to escape, clearing their eyes with their khaki sleeves, eyes burning from the burning. Mick was smart enough, strong enough, to dodge the maimed bike among the dead horses, over the rubble from the collapsed façades, through the squishing guts of the dead men, sticking to the smoke. The alley wasn't far, closer and closer, until a Lee-Enfield bullet ripped through his thigh.

Mick Kavanagh didn't make a sound. The pain was far too intense to open his clenched teeth. They swung through the narrow opening of the lane just as an indiscriminate artillery round collapsed the entry. At least they wouldn't be followed that way. The two Kavanaghs were entering a Dublin unknown to them, unknown to the likes of Padraig Pearse, even Michael Collins—then. The world of the starving, the waifs, drunks and whores of the slums who had crawled out of their Liffey sewers to see what they could scavenge from the blasted shops. Rheumy eyes and bloody lips watched and called to them, more for food than damnation—or praise. The poor had nowhere to go, and they bore the fires and the shelling like yet another preordained visitation of privation. Dumb as cattle.

Mick stopped the motorcycle in a dank alleyway, pulled off his tie and cinched it around his thigh. The bullet had taken a chunk of flesh with it when it passed through. There was a lot of blood, but he wasn' completely hobbled—on the bike, at least. Very close through the murk, low smoke over damp slate, the brothers could see a small fire, a cooking fire. Around it huddled, dimly, like bundles of rags, women in black shawls, the "shawlies" of the streets, and their broods of children, tubercular, noses running, lice infested all. Standing above them, a priest in his long soutane and stovepipe hat. He looked at the brothers, dark anger on his face, his voice stern, condescending as he walked to them. "You people have no right to do this. I forbid it. Come with me now. Surrender to the authorities. I'll give you the absolution you need. Get off. Kneel. Pray."

Danny Kavanagh raised two fingers in an obscene salute. Just as they started away into the night, he turned his bandaged head to the priest. The voice a mummy's croak: "Fuck off, priest. We'll not be needing the likes of you." The priest watched them disappear, shock, disbelief, outrage on his face.

"Christ, Danny, it'll be hell for you, that's certain." His brother snapped back, "Horshite. And so?"

3. Cromwell's Ghost

"Ah, that's a good man, yerself. Saved me life, so. No milk?"

"Stuff it. Yer lucky enough to get a cuppa tay out here among the spirits. Should douse the fire. No tellin if the walls have eyes—and noses—in this evil smellin place. Faery's round about here, no lie, Danny," Mick said, looking over his shoulder. "Least we're outta the wind."

"Right, right. Up the banshee, I say. Damn the damn birds, anyhow. Don't they ever shut their gobs?"

"Guess not. Tryin to wake the dead, maybe. Or turn us in. Or shake old Cromwell up outta the grave so he can come back to Drogheda for another go. Left some of the old buildings standing, lucky for us, the crazy Prot."

"Lucky, indeed. If we didn't find St. Laurence Gate in a hurry, we'd never have found the Sunday Gate up there on the bank or the old fella's digs, neither. Near thing, wasn't it?"

"They were on us like flies on shite, alright. No surprise. It was only a matter of time before they knew we had the bike. Shame to leave it. When all this is over, I'm gettin me one just like it; only not so bent. Your fault," Mick said with a small smile.

"Mine is it? Seems to me I wasn't the one drivin into posts and all. Goddamn birds. Shut the fuck up, ye frog spawn."

The brothers sat on an old grave, their backs against an inside wall of an ancient stone church; a ruin now, roofless. It formed the central focus of Monasterboice, a graveyard in the isolated countryside north of Drogheda. The grave's cruciform marker was complete with a crumbling corpus. Nearby, two tall 10th century stone crosses carved with biblical scenes, the remains of an 11th century round stone tower, a hundred feet tall, and a jumble of graves: old, illegible, overgrown, and new, pristine, tended. The grey stone was mottled with dull, green-blue lichen. It was 9:00, and the carrion crows objected fiercely to the coming darkness and the presence of live inhabitants. The wind was constant, ruffling the leaves in sporadic gusts, atonal accompaniment to the irritable cawing.

"Danny, I hope the old mucker got away with it. Some brave he was to tell the IRC they could fuck off and get outta his way so he could take the wagon over here to fetch his gear. Right? I thought we were goners, sure. Especially after they found the bike so near."

"Yeh, some feisty, the old fart. Wouldn't even let em look inside. Course they woulda got shot for their trouble. Close enough for the Webley the Big Fella gave me."

"Put a sock in it, Danny. There were too many of em. They woulda had us, sure as the crows won't be still."

Then they were, completely, if only for a few seconds. The men heard the car's tires on the gravel.

"Now we're for it, Mick. How many?"

Mick Kavanagh dragged himself over to a low archway and peered through it, his cheek against the stone.

"Only two, Danny, peelers with pistols. Head for the tower. If we can get in, maybe they won't have the guts to follow. We'll use the gravedigger's plank."

For protection against Viking raiders, the monks had built the door some eight feet off the ground. Mick leaned the plank against the lintel, and Danny clawed his way up it and rolled onto the tower's rotting wooden floor. Mick tried to follow, but the RIC were closing, and his leg slowed him down. Then the wind caught the plank, and it fell to the gravel with a loud thud. He looked up at his brother, and Danny dropped the Webley revolver to him. Mick crouched behind a tall black headstone beside the tower base. The RIC men had heard the noise and approached the ruined church at a crouch. They poked about in the remains of the fire, still smoking. Then they began a slow, cautious circle, pistols drawn, threading among the headstones, ducking behind the tall stone crosses with their depictions of the crucifixion, Isaac and Jacob, getting closer and closer. The tower's conical stone roof was long gone, and the interior was open to the elements—and the crows. "Shite," hissed Danny, as the crows began pelting him from above with liquid splashes of white. The RIC men were near enough to hear something, they couldn't make out what, near enough to notice the fallen plank.

From the gloom, Danny could see them talking and deciding that heading back to Drogheda for reinforcements would be much better than being shot trying to get into the tower. They turned to go, pistols down, when Mick Kavanagh appeared from behind the headstone like an apparition and shot them both, point blank. Their faces looked surprised as they died. The carrion crows scattered screaming from the trees.

"Jaysus, Mick, you've done them both, that's sure. Why couldn't ye just let em go about their business?"

Mick turned a body over with the toe of his boot. "Recognize this one, Danny boy?"

"Can't say as I do; he's a bit of a mess at the moment. Christ, what a mess," he said, gulping at the blood.

"That's Tommy McKay. Remember him in Cross, eh? What a big man he was then. Him of the 'Outta the way, Paddy, or I'll fetch me whip.' The other one, haven't a clue. I couldn't just let them walk away, now could I? There'd be a hundred Tommies here in ten minutes. Least this way they won't know what direction we've taken—for a while, at least. And we've got their car. Can't drive it far, but we can ditch it up the road, then head out cross country for Tallanstown."

"The hell we will. Why don't we just drive the whole bleedin way?"

"Danny, I think yer mind was touched by that rifle butt. How long do ye think it'll take for them to know their boys are late and their car is missin? Eh? Ye daft twit. Jaysus, man, get a grip."

This was one of the few times in his life that Mick Kavanagh challenged a decision made by his brother.

"Well, now, seems yer right for once. What'll we do with this lot? Over the wall?"

After they stripped the bodies of their weapons, they dragged them to the cemetery's low stone wall and dumped them over into the tilled field that bordered it. They thought about emptying their pockets of money, but decided it was disrespectful to the dead and hard on the relatives.

Mick stood staring at the corpses face down in the dirt, a sad, hurt look on his face. He turned away, then back, to look across the wide valley of the Boyne River that stretched out before them in the last of the glimmering light. The crows were back at their vigil, hurling last curses at the sky.

"So where was it then, Danny?"

His brother pointed south. "That way, Slane Hill. Bloody King Billy and his butchers did their worst there."

"Fuck em. Their time's done." He shuddered. "Let's get far away from this place. Like I said, the Faery's hereabouts. I can feel the *Sidhe* lookin right through me." He stared down at the bodies one last time. "Rest in peace, boys. Had to be."

"Jaysus, Mick, what's the chances?"

"Slim to none, I'd say, Danny. They're takin some of the men off to the side. More feckin peelers."

"They know about the graveyard by now?"

"Like as not. Any way ye look at it, they'd be after anybody got out of Dublin. Especially you, with somebody's night shirt wound round your head like an Ayrab. How is it?"

"Aye, they would, too. And us so close. It's not good, Mick, infected. I'm hot as a poker. You go on yerself. I'll get the bastards' attention."

"Not likely, Danny. Don't think I can gimp around them that fast. If they take us both, so be it. But I'll not be crawling back to Cross on my own."

"Ah, the hero, is it? What you need's a bit of confession. A novena might even save your soul. Me, I need convertin. No more Allah for me."

"Good thought. Shame we ditched the car. Maybe you were right for a change."

It was late Saturday night in Tallanstown, not far, a few short miles, but far enough from Dundalk on the Irish Sea. Market day, and there were many restless, puzzled people from the surrounding farms who should have been home hours ago. They crowded the square in front of the brothers. After fifteen rebels, among them the seven signatories of the Proclamation of the Irish Republic, were executed by firing

squad in the Stonebreakers Yard of Kilmainham Gaol
between May 3rd and 12th, public opinion suddenly swung
very much in favor of the Dublin rising. Saints and martyrs
are the dearest of the dear to the Irish heart. Now, the RIC
and the British garrison across the entire country were on
nervous high alert. Even more troops had arrived to bolster
the forces of Empire in this most distressful country.
Informers' busy whispers rode the constant Atlantic wind.

The side streets were being sealed by troops at the quick
step; bayonets fixed, more marched toward them from
behind. A Crossley tender blocked the road ahead. The
single blue line of heavily armed Royal Irish Constabulary was
backed up by regular British Army troops in combat kit. A
Lewis gun at the ready swept the murmuring crowd from the
back of the Crossley. Locals were let through; any other men
were being herded aside for questioning. Danny's head might
have been badly damaged, but it was on right, and the
Kavanagh brothers turned sharply and pushed through the
heavy doors of a small stone church. A sodality meeting was
underway, and the devout, prominent men of the town were
kneeling in prayer.

Danny Kavanagh was hard to miss. Even though his dressing had been changed several times, in the kitchens of the faithful as the brothers made their way north from Dublin to Drogheda and Tallanstown, a visibly wounded man away from home meant a guaranteed trip to the local jail, then interrogation. It would not be pleasant, now that the two RIC men had been found under a pall of crows in Monasterboice.

They'd been on the run for weeks; their progress slowed by Danny's frequent need to rest and Mick's wounded leg. The brothers had been very careful, moving only at night, sometimes just a few short miles. The old man who took them out of Drogheda in the wagon gave them a friendly Tallanstown address. When they entered the outskirts, they were confident it would be their last before Dundalk and the safety of the IRB, but the house was on the other side of town.

Low talk among laborers, drovers, women in the farmyards, men in the pubs, that they had a message for Big Matt O'Faolain from Michael Collins preceded them. News of the executions and the jailings followed them sporadically. Neither brother was surprised. It had been the same— always. At least Michael Collins wasn't among the dead.

The Kavanaghs knelt in a pew in the dark back of the damp church and bowed their heads. "Christ have mercy, bloody priests," from Danny, as the kneeling pastor stood and turned in front of the altar rail to address his flock: "We all know that many of the rebels against loyal authority have paid the ultimate price for their outrages in Dublin. These were godless men who despised authority, the authority of church and man and king. I admonish you, therefore...."

Behind him, an old, stout woman appeared in the vestry door, her black shawl hiding her face in the soft, candle lit mahogany murk. She blessed herself rapidly, genuflected quickly and blurted out in a high, cracked voice: "Begging your pardon, Father, but it's happenin again, right there in the window of Mrs. O'Shea's shop. It's a miracle, they say. You should come now, so." She turned and disappeared.

The pastor was a youngish city man, educated by Jesuits at Maynooth, and no fool. Even so, he could not ignore what was being said about Mrs. O'Shea's. Faith, in any form, was acceptable to him so long as the church oversaw it. Besides, he knew his parishioners well after five years as their pastor. Not attending would be a sign of immense disrespect to those certain an Irish miracle was just a matter of time. If he did not preside, the wives would mutter to their husbands about the proud priest from Dublin. The collection would suffer.

"Gentlemen," he said to the sodality in front of him, "It is highly unlikely that the Blessed Virgin has made a special trip exclusively for our benefit, but should the unlikely prove to be God's will, then we should all make our way there in an orderly fashion. The officials in the street outside the main door might not understand our intent, so I propose we adjourn through the vestry."

"Saved," from Danny Kavanagh got a snort of derision from his brother as they followed the devout men of Tallanstown through the vestry and into a dark, narrow, stone passage between the church and the rectory. They stayed well behind as, single file, the local men headed for the lane ahead. The orderly walk turned into a jog, then a sprint, to see what was really happening in Mrs. O'Shea's window.

Mrs. O'Shea's was a Tallanstown institution, as famous for the sweets, tobacco and newspapers, as the religious objects she sold: plaster statues of the Virgin Mary, St. Patrick and the snake, the Infant of Prague, holy cards with Irish saints and a blessing from Rome, catacomb sand in glass vials, horn bead rosaries made by wayward girls, all on display in her window. In a satin lined box was her own rosary, blessed for herself at Lourdes. It was not for sale and left the box only during Easter. In 1916, she had prayed for the hanging of the Dublin rebels.

Mrs. O'Shea was seriously embarrassed for a time that she shared her married name with Kitty O'Shea, Parnell's harlot, but she got over it. Her business shrewdness was legendary in the town, and the priest suspected, with good reason, that these sporadic reports of the crying Virgin Mary statue were staged to increase traffic. If so, the strategy worked. The narrow, dead-end, cobblestoned lane was thronged by men and women on their knees, all looking with upraised faces toward her window. At the open end of the lane, the RIC watched resolutely. Orders were one thing, faith another. Not a one of them would let British soldiers disturb an Irish miracle. The Catholic Irish among the troops blessed themselves automatically.

Danny and Mick Kavanagh fell to their knees as well, across the lane from the window. Mick grunted from the pain in his thigh. Men and women poured into the street, the whites of their eyes prominent in the oil-lit gloom, searching for a statue they could not possibly see. The decade of the rosary began with the priest's deep voice; the crowd took it up. A man and a woman pushed through the crowd and fell to their knees beside the Kavanaghs. "Shite," said the man, the shorter of the two, as he lifted his knee and bent his head to stare at the smeared, fresh leavings of a dog. "The wife will be some happy about that."

The tall woman with him was a shocking sight, wearing britches like a Protestant, and a broad soft hat that shadowed her face. She took an exaggerated sniff at her partner's distress and flashed a small, satisfied smile. In the glow from the street lamp, Danny could see the teeth were good. "There, there, Eddie, it's in a fine cause. Not every day, Mister Devlin, do you see the Virgin in a sweet shop." She blessed herself.

She turned to Danny Kavanagh. "Come for a miracle, mister? Maybe Mary will heal that head of yours."

Danny mumbled, "So, kicked by a horse. Never hurts to ask." Under his coat, his hand tightened on the butt of the Webley revolver the Big Fella himself had given him. The one from the RIC man Mick killed was stuck in his belt.

Still annoyed at the mess on his trouser leg, Eddie Devlin looked directly at him, then turned to Mick. "A horse is it? In

Dundalk, we heard most of the horses in Dublin were dead, like many of our people. But there's talk about a real miracle down there, sure. Two eejits got out on a motorbike. Kavanagh, the name would be, two thieves from Crossmaglen. That wouldn't be your honors, now, would it, so? On your way to Dundalk for some sea air?"

Mick put his hand on Danny's arm, knowing exactly what his brother was thinking: shoot both the spies, then get away in the confusion. "Now why would a couple of country men be going to Dundalk instead of home? We've no relatives there, as it happens."

"Oh, aye, not likely two Crossmaglen lads would. Their relatives are mainly of the grazing persuasion. But we've heard you might be after seein one grand man of the town: Big Matt O'Faolain himself."

He dropped the banter and the pleasant tone: "Look, boys, we've been sent to get you there. You've no chance in hell of gettin outta this, else. They found your motorbike outside Drogheda, then the RIC car you ditched, but all the bastards here know is that you're on your way north. Don't know what you look like—yet. You'll be on a ship to a Brit jail right smartly if you don't come with us. What's it to be, then?"

Danny's hand came out from under his jacket and said to his brother: "Well, boyo, I guess they've got us. You think?"

"They do, Danny boy, they do. I've always wanted to take the sea air in Dundalk."

"Right, then," from the woman. She folded her hands in prayer and said in a reverent whisper, loud enough only for those nearby to hear: "I see her. It's the Virgin Mary come to us. She's crying. Look, she's crying for all of us. For Ireland." Her visitation quickly spread from the back to the front of the hopeful supplicants. Suddenly, the crowd began to sway forward on its knees; a few people in the middle jumped to their feet and made for the window; then the surge was on. Even the priest, standing with his arms out, could not stop the press of believers.

The four of them walked quickly down the street, away from the window and the RIC. The woman in the scandalous britches knocked on a narrow red door in the continuous line of cramped houses. It was opened quickly by a dirty, unshaven man with his suspenders dangling at his sides. He said nothing, simply stepped aside to let them through. As the four rebels crowded past the wife and children eating at the small kitchen table, one little boy held his nose: "That's a right stink that is." The man with the foul breeches considered giving him a backhand until his partners pulled him through the back door.

Outside, they stepped across the tiny, trash strewn yard, swung aside the rickety gate and walked down the common laneway, pushing three bicycles that were left for them against the brick wall. Eddie Devlin swore, "Christ Almighty, supposed to be four." The woman blessed herself again and said, "That was a sin, what I did back there. I hope you two shoneens appreciate that. Farther Murtagh will have my guts for garters."

"Now it's the nun in britches is it?" Danny was definitely amused by this brash and reckless woman. "Now, where's *your* bicycle, missis? The men have theirs. I guess you'll just have to ride the bar in front of me then." That was about all he had left for bravado. Only Mick could see he was starting to sink to the slate, so he held his arm firmly. He knew Danny wouldn't want to show the pain in front of the woman.

She tore the bicycle from Danny's hand with a snarl. "If you think I'm riding all the way to Dundalk in front of some one-eyed pagan, you're not in your head, mister. I'm no nun, that's certain. I'm in the *Cumann na mBan*, alright, but I take no orders from the likes of you, hero or no. Up you go then. The things I have to do for Ireland. Save us all. And don't drop the Webley." On the ride to Dundalk, it was as much as she could do to hold Danny Kavanagh on the bicycle. He didn't pass out, but he was becoming seriously delirious. For Mick, the pedaling opened the wound in his thigh. True to form, he said nothing.

"My God, Mary, what is it when it's at home?"

"A Kavanagh, brother to the Mick outside. And a shame that. He was a handsome devil once, Sophie. You should just hear the blasphemy from the cheeky mouth on the man. He's a pagan, sure. A dangerous one, at that."

"I suppose. But he's still so. Once it heals. I think it makes him look a bit of the noble. He hasn't spoken since you got him here?"

"Sister, next you'll be feedin the cats in the yard again. Just look at him then. But no, not a sin out of the mouth yet."

Sophia O'Faolain did look, and winced as she cleaned the suppurating wound and began to rebandage the head of the unconscious Danny Kavanagh. A country girl, no stranger to damaged men, her reaction had less to do with the wound, than because her older sister, Mary, had a habit of being right. Both were fervent women, in religion and in their devotion to the *Cumann na mBan*, the women's division of the Irish Volunteers. The *Cumann* leader, their magnificent heroine, Constance Countess Markievicz, was second in command to Michael Mallin at St. Stephen's Green during Easter week. Word spread quickly among the *Cumann* that she took credit for much more than the green flag that flew over the GPO next to the Irish tricolor. Her Mauser rifle-pistol was just as effective as the weapons of the male Volunteers. Everyone knew she kissed it reverently before surrendering it. Markievicz was under sentence of death in Kilmainham Gaol, caged alongside her rebel cohorts. Both O'Faolain women idolized her and the other brave women who fought the English. Mary wore the britches in imitation of the Countess, even though Markievicz was an upper class Protestant. Sophia was the more demure of the two, preferring the fashionable high necked blouses and long skirts made from Irish wool.

At first glance, it would be difficult to tell they were sisters. Mary, twenty-two, tall, willowy, thin, with her dark red flame of a mane and sharp tongue, had turned into a sophisticated suffragette, a believer in Jim Larkin's workers' state. A woman of the 20th century. Sophia of the hushed voice, voluptuous body and long hair worn in a bun, was committed to the cause but torn by her deep religious belief, her traditional need for husband, family. Hers was the Ireland of the 19th century, the isolated, painfully beautiful *Gaeltacht* and all it stood for. Her world was defined by Queen Maeve and the heroic *Cúchulainn*, the folk tales and poetry of W. B. Yeats, Maud Gonne, Lady Gregory. The pale skin of her nineteen-year-old face and the dark blue eyes were startling beneath the white banshee flash in her shining black hair. Like her sister, her fuse was short, her temper hot but fleeting. Once committed to something, the O'Faolain sisters did not let go—ever.

"It's no good, girls. Somebody has a big mouth. They've probably just heard a rumor, mind, but the RIC is likely to show up sooner rather than later. Besides, there's a fat reward for anybody turns in a Shinner, especially our distinguished guests, so no good taking chances. Sophie, you show our two Armagh friends the house down in Blackrock. Eddie, take a few of the lads and go with her. Mary, you'll be coming with us. It's just not as safe as it was, so we should split up."

Mary O'Faolain knew better than to say anything. Despite her acceptance of the chain of command, she resented the idea of being ordered to do anything. Matt O'Faolain was her father, though, and did not tolerate back talk from anyone, especially the daughters. Sophia, on the other hand, obeyed immediately, convinced of the rightness of the plan.

"Sophie, where's the brother, then?"

"My name is Sophia, Mister Kavanagh, and don't you forget it. You're to call me *Miss* O'Faolain, if you please. I'll not tell you again."

"Of course, marm," he said tugging his forelock and bowing his head. "So where's the brother then, Sophie?"

"Christ have mercy. He's down the road, across there, see, at the garage, working on the lorry. We have to move the arms further out of town, but we'll not get far in that contraption the way it is. Will he fix it—*Mister* Kavanagh?"

"Oh, aye, that *Mister* Kavanagh can fix anything on wheels. Bank on it. When are we to leave then?"

"When my father gives the order, about two days. It'll be a shame to quit this place. Lovely, so near the sea like this. It's beautiful, don't you think? Not so fine as Tourmakeady where I'm from, though."

"Ah, right, the West, land of wind, rain and nervous sheep. Very scenic."

"Mind your tongue, man. I suppose Armagh is better, is it? Land of smugglers and poachers and thieves and pagans. That's enough. It'll be time, then, for the stitches. Maybe that will stop your mouth for a bit."

"My family and I are deeply honored," he said with a deep bow, right arm across his stomach. "The stitches? Oh, I suppose. Tell Eddie Devlin to fetch the sawbones."

"I can't. He seems to have disappeared. No one's seen him since yesterday. Not that I mind. He should keep his eyes to himself, his mind out of the gutter and his thoughts on his wife. Besides, it's not safe. The doctor here in Blackrock is a Protestant. Nobody seems to know what his politics are. It'll have to be someone else."

"Devlin? That slimy little minger. He wouldn't dare while I'm around, if he fancies breathing. Be sure of that," he growled, a dark, lowering look on his face. "For the stitches job, can't think of a better set of hands than your own, *Miss* O'Faolain."

"That day, sir, will never come."

With a wry smile, Danny Kavanagh looked across the road to his brother. Mick stood, wiping his hands on a rag, waved, then pointed to the truck and gave the thumbs up. Danny waved back. He was feeling much better after a few weeks in the old Blackrock house. The 18th century moldings, the turned oak furniture, the high, multipaned windows appealed to his sense of symmetry and fine cabinet work. Sea air, regular meals, rest, and the kind ministrations of the lovely Sophia O'Faolain had done their work. He found her fascinating; difficult, headstrong, but fascinating, a thorough mix of the country lass and the revolutionary woman. And a mind of her own. "It's the eyes," he thought to himself one day as they strolled along the shore of Dundalk Bay. "Now, the rest of her isn't half bad either." The infection had cleared, the bandage came off, and it really was well past time for the stitches to be slipped out of the purple gash in his face.

Sophia stood by him at the window, regarding his profile. It was a good face, the strong face of a strong man. She watched the sadness sweep over his eyes. The wound, touching it, tending it, cleaning it over the weeks, made her romantic nineteen-year-old heart warm to him. Danny Kavanagh was becoming her breathing image of Ireland, damaged, beaten down, but still proud, still handsome. The agony of *Cúchulainn* cast in bronze. If only he wasn't such a one with the words. Or, perhaps, because he was such a one with the words: always the quip, the laugh, the refusal to be serious or worried. His faith, or lack of it, that was an entirely different matter. Somehow, she thought, he ignored the damage to his face. She decided it was due to bravery.

He turned to her and said quietly, looking into her eyes. "Tell me, lass, was the letter sent?"

"Yes, Danny, it was. One of the men went to Crossmaglen on Monday. By now, Jack's wife knows what happened to him and that you two are safe. I've asked Father Murtagh to say Mass so Jack's soul can rest."

"Ah, that." He turned his face from her. "Jack's soul won't rest until we drive the *Sassenach*—the English bastards—into the sea, no matter what the priest does."

"You blaspheme, as usual, *Mister* Kavanagh. How many times do I have to say it? Father Murtagh is one of us. He believes in the cause just as much as you do. You, you heathen, should practise your faith, not always look for ways to mock it."

"My faith? That's rich. Where's the church's faith in me? It's never done a damned thing for me or mine, except tell us how wrong we are, how we should bow down to church and landlord, then pay them both. Alright, alright, I have to say Father Murtagh seems a fine man, even though he is a priest. But don't go on with the men are different from the institution again. It doesn't wash with me."

"Finally. Perhaps there's hope to get some religion through that thick skull after all if you can see Father Murtagh for what he is at last."

He turned back to the window, his anger subsiding. "It's a good thing the skull is thick, *Miss* O'Faolain, otherwise I'd be denied the pleasure of this particular piece of theology."

Danny looked back to Mick. He was leaning against the side of the lorry, lighting his pipe. Mick looked up, smiling, and waved again, just as two Crossley tenders thundered around the corner and skidded to a halt between the house and the garage. Soldiers and RIC spilled out, Lee-Enfields and pistols at the ready. Mick looked to his brother and made a cross with his fingers, then disappeared into the dark interior of the garage. Danny understood immediately that Mick would be heading for Crossmaglen as fast as he could.

Danny grabbed Sophia's hand and pulled her to the back of the house. On the way out the door, he snatched the Webley from the table and stuffed a box of shells in his pocket. "The church, Danny. We'll be safe there." "Christ have mercy, bloody priests," Danny said as they ran along the beach, hand in hand.

"Right, you two in here, now. They wouldn't dare." Father Murtagh herded them into the tiny penitent side of the confessional. Sophia had to perch on Danny's knee. Hurriedly, the priest draped the purple stole around his neck, just as a British corporal and two privates crashed through the door. "Gentlemen, please, this is a church. You can't just burst in here like that. Weapons in sight of the altar? God save us. It won't do. Besides, there's no one here except old Mrs. Curran for confession. It'll be on your heads if she dies of a heart attack. Out, lads, out. And come back for Mass later without the guns."

The corporal pointed his bayonet at Father Murtagh's chest. He had a strong English Midlands accent, and he was well aware he was in Cromwell country. "Forget that, priest. Stand aside. We're after two Shinner bastards, a woman and an Armagh man with a scar on his face. We have to look. Orders from a higher authority. Out of the way."

In the confessional, Danny Kavanagh had one arm around the slender waist of Sophia O'Faolain. He could smell the sweet soap in her hair. She looked down at the hand on her waist and memorized the strong pattern of proud veins in it. With the other, he pointed the Webley at the pierced door panel, steady, waiting.

She was completely correct in her assessment of Father Murtagh. Saintly, devout, patient, devoted to his people and his faith, perhaps, but he was also a red faced, burly man in his forties born of northern farming stock and active in the Gaelic Athletic Association. Many a head had fallen to his hurley stick. He had no liking for the English in his land. In the seminary, he had looked deeply into his soul and could find no contradiction in his dual loyalty.

"Well, my son, you'll have to use that to get by me. Part of my vows, you understand, no hard feelings. I'll pray for you." He gave the man the sign of the cross.

"None a yer mumbo jumbo, ye papist bastard. Out of the way, I'm tellin ya."

The two privates were Catholic, Irish, and completely terrified. One of them plucked up his courage. "Jaysus, Johnny, that's a priest. You can't go stickin a priest in his own church. There'll be a riot. Let him be, can't yez? There's nobody here, anyway. And if the father says there ain't, then there ain't. Come on lad, let's get us a drink. The rest of us'll find the Shinners soon enough."

The corporal wheeled angrily on the private, thought better of it and laughed. "Right, a bit of the black stuff. That's the ticket. Lead on." He turned back to Father Murtagh, snarling. "Don't forget, priest, you see them Sinn Fein rebels, you tell us quick. Got that?"

"You'll be the first to know, corporal, may Saint Polycarp forgive me if I don't."

On the way out the door, the corporal asked his men, "Who's this Saint Polycarp, then?" The courageous one piped up, "Haven't a clue, corp. Where's a pub in this town?"

Father Murtagh turned to the confessional door. "They're gone for now. You two stay there until I tell you the coast is clear."

It was Sophia's voice. "Father, is there really a Saint Polycarp?"

"Just popped into my head, lass. He was a martyr, betrayed by his servant. I'll be back, shortly."

They could hear his quick steps nervously echoing to the front door of the church. "Now, *Mister* Kavanagh, you needn't hold me that tight. I'm not after falling down. And tell the truth, when's the last time you were in the confessional?"

He held her tighter. "Time out of mind lass, time out of mind. I can smell it, though, that's sure."

"And what would that be, now?"

"Brimstone, the fires down below. I'm saved at last."

She slapped his hand. "Shush, Danny. We're in church, remember?"

"Aye. Do you think we can find out what's become of one Eddie Devlin?"

"He shouldn't be that hard to find. Rather fond of the bottle. Why?"

"I'm thinkin of Saint Polycarp and the servant, Sophie. That little weasel turned us in for the reward. Had to be him. How else would the Tommy have known about me?"

"True, Danny, true. Should we tell my father? He'll throw him out of the IRB in a second. Sad, though; it will ruin him around here."

"No sense bothering the man. I'll have a chat with him myself, personally."

"It's hard, Danny. Are you sure it's him? What will you do if it is?"

He thought for a long second, deciding what to say, what not to say. "I'm pretty certain. Yes, it has to be. We've been betrayed by people like him for too long. If we're to win, it has to stop—now."

They could hear Father Murtagh's steps returning to the confessional. The clicks of leather on stone were light, measured, unhurried. She was looking down, her face turned into his shoulder, a sad frown on her face. Danny Kavanagh laid the Webley on the floor, put his hand on her cheek, turned her to face him and kissed her cheek quickly, in reassurance, not desire. She could smell the gun oil on his hand.

4. "Merry Ploughboys"

Two days they hid in the church as the RIC and army sweep widened away from the town. Wisely, Father Murtagh said nothing to Danny about religion. He knew full well he had a renegade on his hands, but he was worldly enough to bide his time. Danny was relieved. Besides, he didn't want to show disrespect for a man who had risked his life for him—for her—and taken out the stitches with a steady hand and an impassive face. Sophia felt the palpable tension between them. "Men are such odd creatures sometimes," she thought. Kneeling at the altar rail, she prayed to Mary Magdalene for the repose of Jack Kavanagh's soul, the repatriation of Danny's and forgiveness for a future she feared.

On the afternoon of the second day, Big Matt O'Faolain strode into the church, a large stone block of a man with a square, bristling jaw and bushy red eyebrows like flaming brambles. He was flanked by two men in dark, heavy suits. The jackets were oversized, but they didn't hide the bulges under their arms. He took one long look at his daughter and Kavanagh, and turned a dark, thunderous glare through the brush of his eyebrows in Sophia's direction. She blushed. Father Murtagh smiled.

"Father," O'Faolain nodded in the priest's direction, "thanks for your help the other day. You've earned the right to hear what I've got, if you choose, but forgive the rush, we don't have much time." The priest bowed his head.

"Fine, then. Danny, I've had a long letter from the Big Fella. Amazing how quickly he got around the guards. He's in Frongoch Internment Camp in Wales with the rest of the boys. Says it's the best place on earth to reorganize the IRB. Word has it that a lot of the lads will be let out come Christmas, but probably not the likes of Collins or Mulcahy or McKee. Or de Valera, for that matter, being the only Commandant who wasn't shot, and all. Lucky for him he's got Yank citizenship. Anyway, part of the letter has to do with you and your brother. He wants you back south, in Dublin, to work with our people there and prepare for his return. Mick got back to Crossmaglen yesterday, and Collins wants him to stay in South Armagh and head up the Brigade there. What he says is that there'll be plenty of men back from the trenches with scars of all sorts, and you won't be marked much in the city. Makes sense. They'd know about you quick enough if you showed up in Crossmaglen.

"You South Armagh boys have the reputation for bein a law unto yourselves, but I hope I don't have to remind you we're still at war. These are IRB orders, not requests. By the way, I'm empowered by the Big Fella to give you the rank of Lieutenant. Seems some bright light in Wales came up with the name Irish Republican Army, so that's what we're called now, and that's what you're in. You'll be wanting some time in Cross to settle your affairs and say your goodbyes, no doubt, but it'll have to be quick, in and out."

"Thank you, sir. I'm honored. Truly. I would like to go back home for a bit. No doubt I'll need to make a living in Dublin, so I should get my tools while I'm there. One request, though. I've a bit of business to clear up here before I leave. It should only take a day or two."

"You sure? I could take care of it, but it's your decision. Entirely up to you. Not too much noise, though, got it? We don't want to stir up the RIC and the Tommies again."

"Quiet's the word, sir."

The two men shook hands. Danny was left with a piece of paper in his hand. He did not register that he had it, just slipped it into his pocket. Father Murtagh and Sophia both had a very good idea what it was. Of the two, only the priest knew what would happen. It saddened him—for Danny, for Sophia.

The note had the name of a pub, The Four Chimneys, and a location, on the outskirts of Inniskeen, a few miles inland, on the Fane, a salmon river of some repute. Matt O'Faolain made a car available, with one of his men, the ancient Fenian Tom Malloy, as the driver, but he didn't tell Danny about the passenger: his daughter, Sophia.

"No, that's flat. You've no business in this, Sophie. This is a job for the men. What if you're caught, then? I'll not be spending my time saving a woman when there's work on."

"The men is it? Ever been to Inniskeen, *Mister* Kavanagh? I thought not. Neither has old Tom. He's from Newry. You'll not know that it's Devlin's home town, either. Or that he has more than a brother or two. Or that he has his lads with him. He might be a little weasel, as you put it, but he's no pushover, that's sure. You'll be needing me. Besides, it's orders. You still follow orders, Lieutenant?"

"Bloody hell—beggin your pardon, marm. I guess it'll have to be. Just stay in the car."

By the time they got there, it was 9:30 on a mild Thursday night in early July; the rain had quit, and the northern light had turned such a dense mercury silver they could almost rub it between their fingers. The pub stood on its own, a quarter mile from the town center. It was packed with men from the surrounding farms; the married couples in the snug. There was music from a fiddle and a squeezebox, loud, not very melodious. Old Tom, the driver, went in to reconnoiter and have a quick wet. They had two hours until closing.

"This will be hard, Sophie. We'll have to wait until the place closes and he weaves off to bed. I'll find him then."

"Oh, think, man, think. He lives with his brothers and his wife and all at the family place, about a half mile from here. He'll be weaving off with his lads by his side. No, we need to draw him away by himself before closing. I know this place. Outside, in the back, there's tables where the couples sit in fine weather. I'll go in with old Tom, find an outside table, order a shandy, and bat my lashes at Mister Devlin. It won't take long."

Danny thought for a moment. He had to admire her practicality, her bravery, and he knew arguing would not make a dent in her resolve once she had set her course. He feared for her, but in his mind he was a soldier at war; she was a soldier at war. "Right, then, I'll be near, just draw him off far enough so nobody will hear." He hadn't decided what to do, exactly, with Eddie Devlin.

She was right. It only took a few minutes for word to reach Eddie Devlin that the divine Sophia O'Faolain was gracing a table at The Four Chimneys. He was well into the Jameson by this time on a Thursday, comfortably drunk and completely at home, spending freely from the reward. As far as he knew, no one was aware of his betrayal of the Kavanaghs. Once the RIC and the soldiers showed up in Blackrock, it was only natural for all of O'Faolain's men to split up and head for home until things quieted down. Even so, he wasn't drunk enough to let down his guard. One look at her swelling blouse, though, and his groin began to stir.

"Well, now, lass, it's fine to see you here. Right smashin as always. What brings you to the wee town of Inniskeen?"

"We're just on our way back from Carrickmacross. My father wanted me to pay for some heifers he bought there. Old Tom and I decided it was a dry trip, so we thought to stop for a bit of refreshment."

"Right. What'll yez have? My treat, of course."

"No, no, I've got mine, and Tom'll be off for another in a minute or two. It's grand to see you had no problems with the RIC, Eddie, fine lad that you are."

"Ach, none atall. They couldn't find a Devlin at an IRB meeting. Did they get the Crossmaglen boys, then?"

"I don't think so. They've disappeared in any event. The rumor is they're back in Armagh. About time, too, I was getting rather tired of the scarred one's mouth and roving eye."

"Aye, a shiftless boyo, that one, ugly as a farm boot. Are ye off for another tot then Tom? Well away. Have a word with the bartender, Johnny Breen, he's a fine one for the jokes. Now, then, Sophie, it's a bit noisy don't you think? Why don't we just finish our drinks and have a stroll on such a fine night? It's just a step or two. The river will be right lovely, I'm thinkin."

"Well, thank you, Mister Devlin. What a nice idea."

Old Tom stuck his head out the front door and nodded to Danny. He circled the pub and watched as Sophia and Eddie Devlin disappeared into the fading light.

"Now, now, Mister Devlin, hands to yourself, there's a good man. You wouldn't want my father to hear you took liberties, now would you?"

"Don't be daft, girl. You know you want it. Why else are yez here, then?" He grabbed her arm, pulled her roughly into the shadow of the entry to the stone bridge that spanned the river and started ripping at her blouse. As he slobbered on her neck, over his shoulder she saw Danny Kavanagh break the shadows.

Danny poked the barrel of the Webley hard into the beefy side of Eddie Devlin. "Excuse me, Mister Devlin; I need a word with you, down below, by the water. Move." Devlin wheeled with a snarl, but when he saw the pistol and the calm, scarred face of Danny Kavanagh, it changed quickly to a whimper. "Now, now, Danny, there's no sense in all this. I was just havin a bit a fun with the girl. No harm done. No harm. I'll just be off back to the pub then."

"Not tonight, Eddie. Down you go. Sophie, you keep watch up here." The two men marched to the bank of the salmon river that spoke and sparkled in the falling silver of the day. "It's not about Sophie, Eddie. She's her own woman, right enough. It's about you and the RIC, boyo. We had a bit of a chat with one of their more friendly lads. He said it was you told them where to find us. I'll just have what you've got left of the reward." Eddie Devlin's back was to the water. Danny faced him, so only Devlin saw Sophia come down the bank.

Eddie's sodden brain worked as fast as it could, trying to find some strategy—anything—to deny the charge, get away. "Me? Now how would that be? I've been in the IRB, just like you, for years and years. Loyal as loyal, that's me. I'm tellin ye, lad, it's the bitch there did the tellin. Told me she hated your guts. She's a right one, too, we've all had a roll with that one. All that religious shite is just a cover for it."

The barrel of the Webley striped his forehead so quickly Devlin had no chance to duck. "Shut yer filthy gob. Give us the money, then. We know it was you." Danny Kavanagh knew, then, what he had to do.

Fumbling in his pockets, Eddie Devlin started to blubber. "It wasn't personal, Danny, not like that. I just needed the money, see, what with the wife and the wee ones and all. You wouldn't leave the poor babbies orphans, would ye now? Here's the lot. It all turned out alright in the end, didn't it now?"

Danny Kavanagh took the money and got very close to Eddie Devlin's face. He was not angry, more calm, deliberate, certain. It surprised him. "Devlin, if you were a man, I'd shoot you from the front. You aren't. Turn around."

Sophia put her hand on Danny's arm. He flinched, startled at her nearness, and turned to her. She did not know his grim, set face at that moment. Like a shade put over a lantern, his look softened to her. He shook his head and turned back to his prisoner. "Eddie Devlin, as a Lieutenant of the Irish Republican Army, I execute you for treason. You can have a moment to pray if you want."

"Fuck you, Kavanagh. You and your lot haven't seen the last of the Devlins."

Danny shot him in the back of the head. Part of his forehead splashed into the water. The body fell forward, one leg in the shallows. Devlin started to moan, cry out to God, his mother, his legs kicking spasmodically. Danny stood above him, horrified he was still alive. He turned to look at Sophia's crumbling face; her mouth worked, no sound. "Christ," Danny hissed through his teeth, then bent forward and put a bullet through Devlin's temple. The body jerked and lay still; the side of the head was missing and a black pool spread like used motor oil on the bank. The head looked like meat; too much like Jack Kavanagh at Boland's Mill.

Danny wheeled away from the body, fell to his knees and puked in the river, wiping his mouth on his sleeve. "Shite," he muttered to himself. He knelt for a second, looking out over the sparkling current. Then he stood, grabbed a leg, and dragged the body into the water, pushing it forward with his foot. His breathing was rapid, shallow.

"Right, that's done. Come, Sophie, let's move along smartly in case anybody heard." He spoke rapidly, his eyes scanning the shadows. "You just go back and sit a bit with old Tom, calmly as you can. If the peelers tie you to it, you can always say he was drunk, got fresh, you told him off and he wandered off. Likely, though, the people around here will understand well enough what happened and keep their traps shut.

"Are you listening, lass? What did you think I was going to do? Ask him nicely not to turn us in again? Did you hear what he said about you?"

Sophia O'Faolain stood rigid, shivering, shoulders hunched, hands balled into fists, watching the dark hump of Eddie Devlin float away toward the Irish Sea. Danny took her arm and shook it. She fumbled with the buttons of her blouse, trying to close the ones at her throat. They were missing. She wrapped her shawl tightly around her neck and held it there.

Her voice was hollow, just above a hoarse whisper. "I've...I've...never seen a man killed before. It's horrible." Eyes wide, frightened, a rabbit given up fighting the leg snare, she looked at him as if she did not know him. She saw death in his hard green eyes, determined, not the stuff of legend or myth. There was no joy, no victory, in his face. Only the sadness she had seen in the Blackrock house. She reached out and touched his smashed cheek.

"Did you have to? Was it right...necessary? At least you got him to admit it. That was good. But it's the last for me. Never again. I'll do what I'm ordered, but not this. Never again." She blessed herself quickly. "I'll pray for him. And for you, Danny Kavanagh."

He was silent, unable to answer.

The Blackrock house was out of the question. Danny regretted that. He hadn't seen Sophia since he got back from

Crossmaglen. Another, deeper regret. He had convinced himself he'd never see her again. He couldn't shake the image of her horrified face. He set his mind to his duty. Through channels, he was told to stay put and wait for orders. It bored him. The safe house was one of several owned by Count Plunkett, father of the executed Joseph Mary. A circular gravel drive led to a large, two-storey, whitewashed stone house with freshly painted black-green trim and an impeccable thatch roof. It stood facing the water near Gyles Quay on the Cooley Peninsula. Sitting outside it, Danny looked west, out over Dundalk Bay to Dundalk itself. "She's there," he thought. He wondered what she was doing. Who sat by her. Behind him, Slieve Foy rose bulky and shrouded. Nearby, the high, mysterious turf bog on Angseley Mountain kept the secrets of Queen Maeve, *Cúchulainn* and the Cattle Raid of Cooley buried deep. Slieve Foy was draped and swept clean and draped again in sheeting mist. On the stone parapet beside him a bottle of the Irish, beaded with rain, stood unsteadily on the lichen. He had two, quickly, but the third stood by him, untouched. Going home hadn't been easy.

Jack's wife was dry eyed, but the hard resentment in the muscular line of her raw jaw was like a slap. She looked at Eddie Devlin's reward money in her hand as if it had cut her palm. Then the hand snapped shut in a hard fist, farming knuckles red and cracked. "All the Kavanaghs have to learn it's not up to them to save the country, save the world. Damn you, Danny Kavanagh, damn you. You're just like your father, and you'll end the same way. Look what you've done to your face. Jaysus, Mary and Joseph, what a mess," she said as she herded her children back into the house and slammed the door. "Don't be commin back soon," she yelled through it.

He knew immediately she was right about the face. Like most men, for him shaving was both automatic and onerous, something to be got through and done with. He stropped his razor absently, a ritual his father always insisted on after the shave, then toweled off the rags of lather, staring in the mirror. For the first time since Dublin, he had a clear look at himself as others saw him. The scar was large, deep, angry, ugly. "Not a chance, son," he said to himself. "She'd only look twice at you for pity. Then there's the Devlin business. I don't think she really understood that." It was a deception. Neither did he; up close like that with a former comrade was much different from using a rifle or a bayonet in anger on a Tommy. That he could justify.

Saying goodbye to Mick turned into a long drunk. The IRB took them out to an isolated farm in the glens between Crossmaglen and Cullyhanna for two days, a welcome for the heroes of Easter. Danny didn't remember much, except for the final morning after. The brothers stood in the rain by the side of the car waiting to take him to the safe house at Gyles Quay; old Tom sitting patiently behind the large wheel. Mick took his hand. "Danny, we'll kick the bastards out yet. Soon or Never. You watch. Once the Big Fella gets back. We've never had more willing men in the South Armagh Brigade before. Good men, true men. All I have to do is train them. If only we had more guns, like the Thompson we saw at the GPO—right smashin, that. You just do what you must down in Dublin. We'll meet again shortly."

"That we will, no doubt. Soon or Never." Danny's look was not so certain. "Just take my advice, Mick, have a few good men close. Otherwise, watch your back. I'll get a letter home when I can." He started toward the open door of the car, then turned back. "Mick, we have to beat the bastards. Have to. If we don't, it's all been for nothing."

"Like hell, Danny boy, we'll have them on the run by next year. Mark my words."

"Next year," Danny thought on the ride south. "Next year, next year. It's always next year.   How long will it be? Maybe I'll be in the ground before we get our country back. Maybe not, though, maybe not. It all depends on what Michael Collins can do."

He believed that, then. The fate of the country depended on one man still in an enemy jail across the Irish Sea in Wales. He believed it well enough, but he was not easy in his mind.

The rain started in heavier. Gray sheet after gray sheet whipped over Dundalk Bay. Wearily, he picked up the glass and the bottle and headed for the house. At night, the images came: Jack flipping onto his back at Boland's Mill, the sound of his rifle bullet piercing the English helmet, the blood of the men he bayoneted, Mick shooting the two policemen, the looks on their astonished faces, the texture of the hair on the back of Eddie Devlin's head and her angelic face invaded his sleep at will. He was tired, exhausted with the waiting, the delay, the lack of action, justification. He would never admit it, but his wounds, physical and emotional, had not healed.

He stood in the doorway, shaking off the rain, pushing his wet auburn hair out of his eyes with both hands. The car was black, unfamiliar, a bit grand, as it glided slowly over the gravel in the drive. He was alone, no backup, just the housekeeper. Automatically, his hand reached inside for the Webley that sat at the ready on the hall table. He kept it behind his back, watching calmly, waiting for fate.

The rain was pelting now; God's bucket turned over for the greenness of Ireland. A woman and a man jumped from the car and ran toward him. The woman had her shawl over her head. The man held an umbrella in front of his face. "Out of the way, *Mister* Kavanagh. Do you want us to perish in the wet, then?" Sophia O'Faolain and Father Murtagh shouldered their way by him into the hall, turned into the parlor and dropped their wet things in front of the coal fire.

In the door of the parlor, Danny stood, mouth open. The Webley still dangled from his fist. He looked at it as if he had no idea how it got there and quickly dropped it on a cushion.

"Well, now, me first guests. That'll call for a touch of the Irish, I'm thinkin. Back in a tick."

He returned with glasses and the bottle, and busied himself at the sideboard, the scarred side of his face averted from her, collecting his thoughts, trying to hide his pleasure, embarrassment.

"There, now. *Sláinte*," he said in Gaelic. "*Sláinte va*," they responded. "I'm honored indeed to have you here, marm, Father."

Sophia stood tall, her arms straight at her sides, stunned by his manner, so distant, stiff, almost furtive. She put down her glass and walked to him. "*Mister* Kavanagh? If it is you when you're at home. Remember me? Hold still if you please." She took his cheeks in both her hands and turned his head to face her directly. She kissed the battered cheek, then the other. "There, that wasn't half bad now, was it?"

He spun away from her, embarrassed, glowering angrily. "Thanks so much for the notice, marm. So very kind."

The dinner was silent, tense. The housekeeper murdered the beef and undercooked the potatoes. Danny had had too much of the Irish before they sat down. Father Murtagh tried to carry the conversation by reliving a hurley match in Carrickmacross in his youth. Sophia stared at her full plate, open palmed hands crossed on her lap. "Right you are, Father," from Danny. "It's a wonder you can play an Irish game at the same time you and your lot keep the Irish down. You and the popes."

"Danny, I understand entirely why you said that. Let's just say my faith in God and my faith in my country are two sides of the same coin. What the popes, the hierarchy, have done—or not done—over the centuries is really none of my affair, unless they're matters of faith or morals. I'm not a political man—in that sense, at least. They have had their concerns. I have mine: as a priest, as a man. What I do know is that we have to keep the faith if we're to have a civilized country. Now, what you do, or don't do, is entirely up to you. I'd like us to be friends, man, collar or no. As a friend, I have to tell you aren't being particularly manly when it comes to Sophia, here. That's sure."

"Ah, the hell, with it. I'm off to bed, then. The housekeeper will see to your rooms, no doubt. You'll not be leaving this weather." He turned and stomped out.

He awoke in the morning with a dry mouth and a thundering head. Remorse flooded over him. "Ye stupid clot," he said to himself. "They come here to see you—she comes—and you act like a right dumb arse. Christ, what an eejit. Now I've really torn it."

She sat by herself in the parlor, waiting for Father Murtagh to return from his meeting in Omeath. The weather had cleared. She stared into the fire sadly; her hands folded in her lap once more, palms up. Unknown to her, he stood for some seconds in the doorway watching her delicate profile, then came to a decision.

"It's a fine morning then, marm. I hope you have a fine trip."

"Thank you, Mister Kavanagh, very kind, I'm sure." Her voice a whisper.

He walked up to the back of her chair, so she couldn't see his face while he spoke. "Sophie, I'm sorry for last night. Truly I am. It's just that I'll be off to Dublin in a few days. Nobody knows what will happen there—when Collins gets back. I might not be coming north again. I just don't know. Jaysus, woman, what I'm trying to say is that I won't forget your kindness to me, friendship. Father Murtagh, as well. He's a fine man, no matter what I said in my cups. You were good to me—even the way I look now. Even after what I've done and said. I won't forget you, Sophia O'Faolain. I just wish we met—before I looked so bad." He put his hands on her shoulders, bent and kissed her hair.

She stood and spun on him. "Don't you dare. Damn you, Danny Kavanagh, you are such a stupid, blind, vain man. Yes, your face has been smashed. Yes, you drank too much last night. Yes, you said terrible things. Yes, you've had to do horrible things. I was there, remember? How can you talk to me like this? What right have you? What about what *I* think, what *I* want, what *I* see? Is that all nothing? It's plain Mary was right about you. You're a heathen without a drop of regard for anybody in you. Goodbye, *Mister* Kavanagh. Fare thee well in Dublin. Fare thee well. I'll pray you see clearly one day."

On the way back to Dundalk, Father Murtagh at the wheel, the silence was like the silence of death, rich, palpable, with the smell of wet earth. The priest considered what to say, whether to say. Finally: "Sophia O'Faolain. You'll recall, of course, I was the one who christened you. That gives me some rights. You'll recall, of course, I'm your priest, your confessor. You'll have little doubt I'm your friend. So be still and listen to me. This isn't the faith talking. It's me.

"The man's lost in grief, confusion, pain. He's lost his brother. He lost a battle. He probably thinks he's lost his home, as well. No doubt, he's considered that he won't survive very long. He has to come to terms with the Devlin thing. To my mind—the clerical part—he was acting as a soldier. Even though he sought it out himself, he had to do what he did. Then there's the face. He's convinced himself you're only taking pity on him, and that, my girl, would make him furious. Believe me. For a proud man like him, he'd drive you away no matter what he wanted, no matter what you wanted, rather than take chances with your life. My advice to you is not to let him do that. If you want him, that is. And I believe you do. We will plan for the day we can beat some sense into his thick Armagh head.

"And speaking of pride, you'll further recall it's one of the seven deadly sins—in a man *and* a woman."

PART II

SOON OR NEVER

5. TWELVE APOSTLES

"Spare a coin for a veteran, sir? It's a hard rain fallin."

"Certainly, my good man. You'll be needing a bit of the black stuff to ward off the weather."

What seemed such an ordinary exchange between a beggar and a very well dressed, very young gentleman took place on the pavement outside the Turk's Head Chop House at the corner of Essex Gate and Parliament in Dublin. Danny Kavanagh, dressed in his most convincing rags, sat at his usual night time spot, in the shadow of the coal-smoke black walls of Dublin Castle, the large, ancient, deliberately threatening seat of power for the Royal Irish Constabulary and English rule. It was a hive of spies, informers, detectives, men who worked in the dark to keep the powerful in power by making sure the powerless stayed that way. The dungeons were renowned for swallowing the unfortunate.

By day, Danny built houses in Dalkey, south of the city; at his pavement post by night he recorded as many names, movements, contacts as he could without being caught. It was a dangerous business, but Michael Collins needed to know who they were and who they knew. Strangely enough, some of the men he hated most were occasionally quite generous, if condescending, especially when they'd had a few drinks. In the Castle, with appropriate grimaces, they called him "Bootface." Even so, he was careful never to be seen by day and always wore a filthy soft hat pulled low over the eyes of his bowed head. The Webley had worn a comfortable groove under his left arm.

As the crowds swept by in the dark drench, seventeen-year-old Charlie Dolan looked down from under his streaming black umbrella at the scarred man on the pavement as if in concern, pity. "Time to look sharp, Danny. The Big Fella's back again. He'll be wanting everything you've got on these swine. Meeting's tomorrow at Vaughan's Hotel. Nine on the dot; he doesn't like latecomers. And clean yourself up, man." It was early September, 1918, and Danny Kavanagh had been working with the Dublin No. 2 Brigade of the Irish Republican Army since he arrived from the safe house at Gyles Quay. He tried, but he never could finish that letter to Sophia O'Faolain. Here, at least, he hadn't had to kill anyone—not yet. That was a relief.

"Now then, young Kavanagh, it's splendid to see you looking so well. Have a seat, but you had better face the wall. No offence, I trust, it's just that people at the other tables might remember you. Frankly, you've healed up well. You'll not know Mr. Mulcahy on my left, here, or Dick McKee on my right. They were at Jacob's Factory during the Rising, so they missed the fun at the GPO. I've filled them in on your exploits with your brother and the famous motorbike. Ah, grand, finally, the drinks have arrived. About time, too," he said with a familiar bantering nod to the waiter. "Same toast to you as last time, Kavanagh, 'Long life, a wet mouth, and death in Ireland.'"

Michael Collins looked refreshed, invigorated, energetic. The winning way, the friendly, relaxed smile had the required effect on Danny Kavanagh. He knew there was a debt to pay to the Big Fella for getting them out of the GPO. He doubted he could ever repay it in full. It was ironic for Collins to call him young; all four men were in their twenties.

"Now, Danny, first things first. That splendid dandy Charlie Dolan tells me you've become quite the fixture around the Castle. His report says you're very thorough. I'd like your detailed notes, if you please. I'll review them carefully. I hope you won't be offended if I make a few suggestions here and there about future methods.

"You might be wondering about the reason for all this. We've discussed it thoroughly, and we think you should know in detail. The only way we'll ever be successful is if we can shut their eyes in the Castle. They can always send in more troops, but without spies and informers, they're blind. I don't have to tell you, of all people, that informers have always been our Achilles heel. We need as much information as we can get from as many sources as we can find. When the list is finalized, we'll—um—we'll see."

"Here's what I've got, sir. The problem is some of the buggers come in and out by car, and I never get a look. They're the most important ones, and finding who they are is very tough indeed. I have to be very, very careful."

"Yes, Danny, we're aware of that particular difficulty, but we think we can solve it. The name's Mick, if you please, same as your brother. By the way, I'm to say hello from him. I've been appointed Secretary of the National Aid and Volunteers Fund, so I've been traveling about the country in my official capacity, if you catch my drift. Just got back from Armagh by way of Dundalk. Your brother's really coming into his own as a Brigade Commander. We'll be needing his lads soon enough. As usual, though, we're short of modern equipment, but we're working on it.

"You may have heard me mention one Joe McGarrity in Philadelphia. He and the *Clann na Gael* have promised us 500 of those handsome Thompsons you saw at the GPO. I hope they don't forget the ammunition this time—45 caliber is hard to come by hereabouts. Pity they're so out of touch—politically."

Danny's face brightened at the mention of his brother's name. "Did you see the brother now—uh—Mick? That was kind of you indeed. He's a fine man, a true man. You didn't happen to see the O'Faolains perhaps?"

Michael Collins turned on the famous boyish smile and swept the hair from his eyes with a delicate hand, almost like a young woman's. He winked quickly to McKee and Mulcahy. Mulcahy was scowling into his drink. "Certainly. Matt O'Faolain gave me a smashing report on your exploits in Blackrock. I even spoke to a priest up there, Murtagh's the name, one of us. Splendid chap with his head on straight. He knows what's what. I'd pay attention to his views, if I were

you. Seems he saved your rashers, right enough. That's
about it, I think."

Danny pursed his lips and looked at the table, reluctant to
ask directly. "Right, sir," he mumbled into his drink.

Collins and McKee laughed quickly. "Now, now, Danny,
not so glum. I saw Sophia O'Faolain, right enough. Splendid
she is, too. We had a long chat. For her own reasons, she's
decided not to take part in active *Cumann na mBan*
operations. Requested a support role, only. Fair enough.
Not so Mary, though. She makes the old ticker beat, that one.
Not that Sophia isn't divine. Fortunate the man would be who
could turn her head.

"Alright, man, I won't keep you in suspense any longer.
She asked me to tell you that she hopes you're faring well
and beginning to see clearly for a change. Rather cryptic,
what? Her manner was a bit starchy, I must say."

Danny Kavanagh cleared his throat, shifted uncomfortably
in his chair and remained silent. Fortunately, Collins took the
opportunity to signal the waiter for another round.

It was McKee's turn. Along with Collins and Mulcahy, he
was the third member of the triumvirate that reorganized the
IRB in Frongoch Prison. Danny Kavanagh was completely

aware of who he was and that the small, thoughtful looking Mulcahy was just as powerful in the Irish Republican Brotherhood.

McKee began deliberately. His look was earnest, determined, genuine. "I trust I can call you Danny as well, Kavanagh. I think we'll be seeing a lot of each other in the coming months, so I'd like to start on familiar terms, if that suits. I've a few questions I'd like to ask, and I hope you'll be able to answer them fully. Believe me, it's necessary, and I've no intention of making you uncomfortable without good reason. We're in the city to make sure of our men for the coming operations. Mick, here, has told us a lot about you in the GPO and afterwards. To fill it in a bit, I talked to Captain Cullen and Tom Kelly about your time at Boland's Mill. Sorry about your oldest brother. In any case, we hope you're made of the stuff we need."

McKee fell silent as the waiter arrived. He was the biggest of the four men at the table, over six feet, athletic, muscular. The face was finely chiseled, raven dark hair, light blue eyes. His physical presence was imposing enough, but Danny was not prepared for the voice: melodious, rich, the voice of the Pied Piper. It seemed to cast a spell over him immediately.

This was a man Danny Kavanagh could follow and obey. McKee thoughtfully packed his pipe, then passed his tobacco pouch to Danny before continuing.

"Right. You'll enjoy the tobacco, I trust; my own blend. Tom Kelly tells me you're a dead shot, Danny. That true?"

Danny laughed nervously. "Well, perhaps. Back home in Crossmaglen it was my job to deprive the local gentry of as many of their deer as possible, especially come Christmas, so I learned early to handle a rifle. To be truthful, I am a good shot, yes."

"Fine. An honest answer. But I'm not talking about game here, man. How many did you kill at the Mill?"

"Only one for certain, sir. I fired a lot of rounds, but I can't be sure about any others. The old Mauser I had wasn't very accurate, especially after the barrel overheated."

"No, that won't do. Call me Dick, please. We try to be informal, but that doesn't mean there isn't a chain of command, Lieutenant. I'll just try to jog your memory a bit. What about on the Brit barricade?"

"Oh, yes, that." Danny looked at the table again, the images of Jack's death dropping over him like a bloody, suffocating pall. "My memory isn't really sharp there, but I guess two or three. I was thinking about shooting before, not the bayonet."

Nervous, fidgeting, repeatedly looking at his watch lying on the table, Mulcahy interrupted: "That's all well and good, Kavanagh, but what about the Devlin business?" He traced the invisible pattern of a rectangle with his index fingers as he spoke.

Michael Collins raised his eyebrows at Mulcahy, then turned to Danny. "You'll get to understand Mr. Mulcahy's manner soon enough, Danny. He's a bit impatient—a Dublin man's failing—because we have another meeting shortly and he can't stand to be a second behind his time. Upsets his delicate stomach, see? No doubt, he didn't mean to give offence. Let's just continue, shall we?"

McKee resumed. "Yes, well, humph. Danny, look, as I said, we want to be sure of our men. I'd like to know about Devlin, the whys and wherefores, and how you feel about it now."

Danny gave him all the details, only leaving out what Devlin said about Sophia and the fact she was there when he shot him. He finished, finally: "That's about it, Dick. He was a traitor. Tried to turn us in for the money. I didn't think I had any choice. Took the reward money from him and gave it to my brother's widow. Seemed right." Danny did not say how he felt about the killing.

McKee turned to Collins, a puzzled look on his face. Collins waded in. "Now, Danny, it's a fine thing to protect the fairer sex—heroic, mythological—but it's no secret to us that the girl was there. She told me herself and even what the 'little weasel'—your term, I understand—said about her. However...."

McKee began again. "Danny, we don't have much time left tonight. I have to know how you felt about killing the man, close to, a former comrade. Did you hate it? Take pleasure in it? Do you feel right about it? What?"

"Well, to be truthful, I can't say just how I feel about it. I've thought about it and thought about it. Father Murtagh told me before I left Dundalk that he figured it was justified, in the line of duty and all that, but I'm not what you could call a religious man, so that really has no weight. I had to shoot him twice, and I puked after. It's not pretty, sure, shooting a man close up like that. Besides, he was one of us—or was once. Anyway, I'll have to live with it. No, I took no pleasure in it, that's certain. It's not like with the Tommies."

"Yes, Danny, he was one of us once, but it's people like him who have kept us down for centuries. Surely you know that many of the people you're watching are Irish, too?"

"I do, Dick, and it makes me want to spit in their faces for it."

Collins again: "That was an honest assessment, thank you. I spoke to Father Murtagh, and he told me just about the same. Priest or no, Danny, he's an ally. Don't forget it or sell him short."

"Sorry, Mick, but I just can't abide the church, the popes, the whole business. It keeps us tugging our forelocks and on our knees."

McKee answered: "There's a lot of truth in that, Danny, but we have more pressing concerns right now. You'll recall that Tom Ashe is on hunger strike as we speak?" McKee's look was penetrating, as if he wanted to get inside Danny Kavanagh's skull, his soul. "I have to ask. Do you feel you could do it again? With proper authority, of course. With complete assurance of your man. Could you? We'd need you to volunteer."

"Sir, I just don't know. I'd have to think about it. Can I have a few days?"

"Certainly, Danny, certainly. I'm sure you'll come to the right decision."

As the three men stood and shook hands with him, Michael Collins said, "Danny, no matter what your decision turns out to be, we all respect what you've done already. Make no mistake about that. It's just that we need a very special sort of man for a very special kind of business. Don't feel you've let us down if you can't find it in yourself to take the job on. There'll be plenty else for you to do, no matter what." He turned to leave with Mulcahy and McKee, then turned back. "Right, Danny, I'll need your final answer by the end of the month, latest. Done?"

"Done, Mick, I'm yer man."

"Of that I have no doubt, young Kavanagh."

Outside, the three IRB commanders started walking quickly to their next meeting. McKee halted and faced Collins on the pavement. "What's your thought, Mick, is he game for it? We need good shooters with steady hearts and hands."

Mulcahy answered for him, all the while drawing circles in the air with the index finger of his right hand: "My judgment is no. He's from Armagh. Up there, they all think they're a law onto themselves. Your man thinks too much, dead shot or no. My feeling is he can't be trusted without close supervision; exactly what we don't need. Besides, he doesn't seem to have the stomach for it. At some point, we'll have to consider what to do with the squad once operations are over. Mick, I'm still not convinced it's the best way, but I do think you told him much more than he needs to know. Very unlike you. The McGarrity connection has to be protected at all costs, as you well know. Enough. Come, gentlemen, we'll be late."

"A little suspense is good for the soul, Mr. Mulcahy. We aren't catching a train, after all. I still think he's our man, Dick. Remember who he is, where he comes from, who his father was, his brothers. He's as Fenian as O'Donovan Rossa. We could order him, of course, but that won't do. He'll have to come to the decision himself. I just hope we can find enough men like Danny Kavanagh. Don't forget what Padraig Pearse said over Rossa's grave: '...the fools—they have left us our Fenian dead, and while Ireland holds these graves, Ireland unfree shall never be at peace.' I only wish Pearse, rest him, was a better soldier than an orator. As to the squad, we'll have to break it up. I have my own reasons about McGarrity. Lead on, Mr. Mulcahy, lead on, if you please."

Danny left the hotel by a side entrance. On the way to his lodgings, he swept the question from his mind for the time, and, once more, began composing that letter to Sophia O'Faolain. Before him, in his mind's eye he could see her face; smell the sweet soap in her hair. "Not a chance, son, not a chance," he muttered to himself again and again as he passed from gaslight bloom to gaslight bloom along the wet, smoke-black streets. The climb up the three flights of stairs to his tiny room in Eustace Street was weary.

"It's no good, Danny, the Big Fella says no. That's flat. Mulcahy wouldn't have it either. 'Too risky,' he said. What's with him and drawing things in the air, anyway? One of the lads told me his nickname is 'the tic tac man.' Collins said there's no way we can have you in uniform for the funeral. They'll be Castle spies everywhere. You'd be risking your usefulness. Sorry."

"Charlie, have a heart. They'll be thousands of Volunteers out there. How could they pick me out? I'd just be one man."

"It's hardly up to me, is it? I'm just a messenger. And it doesn't do to shoot the messenger. You're the one with the rank. It's orders. I'm to say they're still waiting for your answer."

"All right. Tell them shortly, shortly. Makes my head hurt, so it does."

Danny, at his post by the Turk's Head on the evening of September 28th, was very close to a decision. He felt he wouldn't be able to live with the images he knew he'd store up if he volunteered. The one's he had already were enough. Nothing specific had been said, that was Michael Collins' secretive way, but Danny knew well enough what was in the wind. The only way they could blind the Castle, as Collins had it, was to put out the Hydra of eyes. There was only one way to do that. Danny was astonished at the boldness of the plan. He admired it, knew it had to be, but he didn't think he had the stomach to be among the assassins. Without that, he was useless.

Still, it was hard not to be allowed to march in Tom Ashe's funeral procession. The savage death of the President of the Irish Republican Brotherhood rocked Dublin. He was sentenced to a year's hard labor in the Kilmainham for making what the authorities considered a seditious speech at Longford in July. He refused to wear prison clothes, or do prison work, and he demanded political status. Denied, he went on hunger strike. Prison officials put him in a straightjacket, stuffed a hose down his nose and force fed him. He died of internal injuries on September 27th. The funeral would probably be as large as the one for Parnell in 1893, and the IRB had planned a vigorous and numerous show of Irish Volunteers, even the pardoned Countess Markievicz, who was neither shot nor imprisoned for life, as the judge put it, only "because of her sex."

The door to the Turk's Head burst open, and two men, obviously drunk, lurched out. Danny knew one, the Irish spy Billy O'Neill; the other was new to him, but the burly man in the fine fedora was identifiably English by the clothes and the mouth.

"Why, there's yerself, then," Billy slurred to Danny on the pavement. "There's a good man. Here, have a pint on me, ye poor sod. Do ye good. Come on, Jim, have a heart, too. This is the old fella wounded at the Somme I told ye about. He's not quite right, then, is he?" Billy said pointing to his head.

"What's this piece of dung doing here, sponging off honest men?" The Englishman gave Danny a boot in his side. "Fuck off, you shite. Is this your 'Bootface,' then? He'd be better off in jail or in the ground like that Shinner bastard Ashe will be soon enough. We'll get em all, bloody traitors. I've heard about you, my man, make yourself very scarce while I'm around. Fucking useless bogtrotter. Just like all you Micks."

"Now, now, then, Jim, let's just head off for another round. It's an hour till closing yet. I know a spot over in Nighttown where the fair maidens of Ireland wait—just a few pence."

"Right you are, top hole. First we fuck em cheap, then we shoot em fast. Good sport."

Ashe's body lay in his Irish Volunteer uniform. In his beggar clothes, Danny quickly walked by the coffin then vanished into the vast crowd outside City Hall. He could see the nearby walls of Dublin Castle. The Angelus began tolling from Christchurch Cathedral. Carried out by a uniformed honor guard wearing full bandoliers, Ashe's casket was draped in the Republican flag, then wreath upon wreath upon wreath of flowers was heaped on it. The cortege started the slow march north, toward Glasnevin Cemetery. The Black Raven Pipe Band walked in front of the hearse. A uniformed firing party marched on each side of it, rifles ready. With his sword drawn, an officer marched behind. Then came Countess Markievicz, a revolver in her holster, leading nine thousand Volunteers. Essex Street, Wood Quay, Werburgh Street, Bride Street, all were packed with thousands of mourners, and probably just as many spies, Danny thought.

He heard the buglers sound the last post just as he came up fairly close to the grave. The firing party presented arms and fired. Then, Danny couldn't believe his eyes. Michael Collins in his officer's uniform stepped out of the crowd. The bravado was stupendous. A wanted man in uniform about to address the crowd at one of the most public and dangerous gatherings ever staged in Dublin. As the smoke from the shots drifted away, Collins said in a clear, loud voice: "Nothing remains to be said. That volley which we have just heard is the only speech which it is proper to make over the grave of a dead Fenian." Just as quickly, Collins was gone. Danny scanned the crowd for him. No luck. Briefly, in a flash of red hair, he thought he saw Mary O'Faolain. "Couldn't be," he thought, but then he considered her worship of the Countess in breeches.

Danny felt a hand on his arm. He reached for the Webley, but it was only Charlie Dolan, dapper as always, with a black band on the sleeve of his dark brown tweed jacket. "Danny, the Big Fella wants a chat later, but you'll have to clean yerself up, first. Can't be lookin like that, and you a Lieutenant, especially where we're going. Might be talk. You're near enough in size to my father, rest his soul, so we'll just hop along to my place for a brush up."

It was definitely time to act. The funeral had been everything Collins, Mulcahy and McKee had wanted: spontaneous crowds, no interference from the authorities, a show of force, the public horrified at the barbaric way Ashe had been treated. Like his brothers in arms, Collins was devastated by the death, but the cause was served. The cause must always be served. The Big Fella was definitely ready for a talk with Danny Kavanagh. The girl? Now that was a complication. Collins expected a wrangle with Kavanagh, a winning over of what he knew was the man he needed with his winning ways. The small pub, The Grocer's Arms, was in a quiet, narrow alley in Temple Bar. It was almost empty of patrons, a rare event in Dublin; seemingly everyone in the city was at Glasnevin. Out of uniform, Collins was serenely sipping a small glass of Jameson Irish Whiskey—a permanent replacement for his formerly usual English Bell's—when Danny Kavanagh strode through the door without Charlie Dolan in tow. Collins, never given to shows of surprise, raised his eyebrows slightly, then nodded to the barman for another glass.

Danny sat down. He was well dressed in the late Mr. Dolan's clothes, his auburn hair brushed back from his forehead, the red of the scar less and less prominent now, a deep, wrinkled dent that made his eye droop toward the flattened, out of kilter cheekbone. Danny pulled the chair away, sat down quickly and began. "Right, Mick. Made up me mind. I'm yer man. When do we start? Let's just not discuss it."

There was a small laugh, then Collins beamed the boyish smile and handed Danny his drink. "Danny, I knew we could count on you. That makes twelve. You are hereby christened the last of the Twelve Apostles. Your training with the squad will start tomorrow. We'll get you the best we've got, information, ordnance, everything. You'll be needing something better than the Webley."

"Unless it's an order, Mick, not on your life. It's like an old friend. Maybe I could use something smaller, though, as a back up, like."

"Of course, your choice. You won't be needing the rags anymore, Danny. We'll get you fitted for a proper uniform in good time. Be very straightforward about it, better offer in England or some such, but you should hand in your notice to the builder you've been working for in Dalkey. He's one of us, of course, but I want it done properly and publicly. Hem. Now, as your first duty in your new capacity, Lieutenant, you're to appear in the courtyard of the National Library on Kildare Street at six sharp this evening. Wear the clothes you've got on. You look grand. Here's a few bob. Get yourself a shave and a wash. Got it?"

Inwardly, Michael Collins was sure of his man, but he hoped he had done right.

"Damn the barber," Danny fumed inwardly. "How bloody long can it take to wash and cut a man's hair and shave his face? Even a bent one like mine." He was hustling down Nassau Street with only a few minutes to go. The bell from St. Anne's began tolling the hour as he sprinted around the corner off Kildare and into the courtyard of the National Library. Full tilt, he ran into her and sent her sprawling into a heap of hat and skirts. "Jaysus, missus, sorry about that, my apologies. Here, let me help you up."

"Sure, and yer a great bloody clot of a horse. Knocking people about like that." She pulled her broad, black straw hat from her face to her head. The trailing peacock feather was bent.

They stood, staring at each other, too stunned to speak. A little way off, on a bench under a tree, Father Murtagh sat quietly, reading in his Breviary. If he laughed, they did not hear him.

"That's a fine introduction after so long, *Mister* Kavanagh. Don't know how to write a letter, obviously," she said, trembling lower lip pouting. Her face was red, and a long wisp of black hair had escaped from her bun. Her hat was very crooked. She looked absolutely beautiful to him.

He took her in his arms and kissed her, swiftly, hard, on the lips. The first time he had done so.

"Jaysus, Mary and Jo.... That'll do, Danny, that'll do. The good father will be scandalized," she said with shock in her voice, but her breath was short and her eyes were dancing. She pushed him away roughly, a palm on his chest, then came to him and kissed him on the lips, swiftly, hard. They heard the laugh from the bench and turned to him, holding each other. The priest pretended he had seen nothing and calmly went back to his devotions.

"If you please, *Mister* Kavanagh, take my arm and give me a proper stroll around this filthy Dublin of yours. It's me first time. Least you can do, ye great beast, after knocking defenseless women senseless. I'm to be back here 8:00 sharp. Father Murtagh and I are going to Mass at St. Patrick's. Of course, you're welcome to come, too, if you will. He tells me it's a grand church. Mary probably won't be there. She's at some workers' meeting or other. My father says to send his regards and remember where the right is. You look grand. Oh, then there's to be an evening meal at the Shelbourne. Mary will meet us. Sure you'll come to that? For me? We'll be leaving tomorrow. Train." She was too winded to continue.

He tugged his forelock. "I'll have to take a pass on the Mass, marm, things to do. But the stroll? Certainly, my pleasure. Couldn't be a finer evening for it. Not even raining. A grand feed later sounds just right. The Shelbourne? A bit on the posh side, ain't it?"

He took her arm gently; rearranging her hat with the other hand. She looked for it, but the Webley was missing from under his arm. He felt incomplete, odd, exposed, without it. The barber would have noticed.

"Right, that's better. Can't be promenadin with the prettiest woman in Dublin when she's half dressed. I'd like a word with your Father Murtagh after the meal. Hope he won't mind, after...well...after things happened and all."

She looked up into his face and laid a hand on his scarred cheek, a hopeful, bright look in her eyes. "Nay, lass, not in his official capacity. I just need to talk to a man I can trust. Someone who's not so close to all this. And brother Mick is in Armagh."

The September evening was fine for Dublin: breezy, low white clouds scudding across the city, driven west to east.

Slowly, they strolled down toward St. Stephen's Green. Except for his comments on the more interesting buildings they passed, anything of importance was avoided. They sat on a bench by the pond and watched the black ducks dabbling for a meal. She tried to be as bright and friendly as she could. Her father had told her little, but she knew things were going to get very, very bad in Dublin. Smiling, she said softly, without the usual bantering emphasis on his name, "So, Mister Kavanagh, what have you been up to all this time? Not writing letters, obviously. Perhaps some Dublin girl has turned your head?" She regretted it immediately. There was a brief flash of panic in his eyes, then something else. "I've made him angry. Twit," she said to herself.

His manner became very stiff, formal. "Actually, *Miss* O'Faolain, I've been building houses down in Dalkey. Even managed to save a bit, what with my night time duties. Don't have much time for the ladies down here. Anyway, they all think they're made of gold. Besides, just look at me."

"Ah, so you've been trying then? Just like a man." In turn, her anger rose, beyond her control. "Will you stop with the poor mouth, poor me? You look like a puppy that's been kicked. There's nothing at all wrong with your looks, *Mister* Kavanagh. Get over it. You should be proud, not duckin yer head like some beggar man on the street."

"Right, well, ah, as to that...."

"Put a sock in it, Danny. There's a good man. I've been worried sick about you, ye dumb clot. When I didn't hear and didn't hear, I talked to your brother in Crossmaglen. Even tried to speak to Jack's wife, but she didn't want any part of it. My father won't tell me anything. What is it? Are you in danger? What? Don't forget I'm still serving, so I have some rights as a soldier."

His face softened: "Shush, now lass, there's a good soul. I'm not allowed to say much. What I can tell you is that since I've been down here—left Gyles Quay—I've been working more or less directly for Michael Collins, kind of gathering information for him. Sorry I didn't write. Honestly. Didn't know what to say. Thought you wouldn't want to hear from me. The way we parted and all. It's just that now, now I've volunteered for a job that might turn out to be a bit risky, and.... Oh, damn, now Sophie, don't do that."

She was weeping. Through it, she said: "Damn you, Danny Kavanagh. You couldn't just join the Irish Volunteers like everybody else. No, not you, the proud Fenian. You had to go in with the Brotherhood, with all their secrets and plots and murders. You'll be dead, and where will I be without you, you stupid man?"

"What in hell is this? You mean to say...? You're mad. I didn't know. Jaysus, you are mad, woman, no lie. This just can't happen now. I mean with what's coming up, it's just not...."

"I don't give a damn about the IRB, Danny Kavanagh. I only give a damn about you. You better say it soon, or I'll dent the other side of yer face so you'll match."

6. SECRET WAR

"Well, Danny, did you, or did you not?"

"I already told you, Father, I said I loved her. She said the same to me."

"It's about time you came to your senses. Honestly, man, I'd given you up for a hopeless dolt. But that's not what I mean, and you know it. I've known her since before she was born, and you're making her life a misery just now. Be a man. Do the right thing by her."

"I couldn't. Can't. Wouldn't be fair. Just hear me out first."

"In my official capacity? Is this a confession?"

"No, sorry, Father, it isn't. I'd—ah—like to speak to you as a friend, man to man, if you will. I think you'll understand. I just don't know what to do. Besides, I'd need permission, and I don't think I'd get it from the Big Fella right now."

"No, he wouldn't give it. We've talked. That's how I got you to Kildare Street in the first place. It would be better if you called me Jim for the time being, unofficially and all."

"Thanks. I'd like that."

The two men were sitting over after-dinner drinks in the Shelbourne Hotel's Oak Bar. Sophia and Mary had departed for the night, more than abruptly. Earlier, during the meal, Sophia was alternately ecstatic, depressed, angry, overjoyed, furious. The shades on her face shifting from red to white and back again. "Why didn't he ask, the stupid man?" she thought. "Maybe he's just toying with me. No, that's not it. I don't understand him; no question there."

At first, Mary O'Faolain was happy for her sister, because she knew where her heart lay: with a husband—this tribal Kavanagh wild man—and children. Politics was out; the military was secondary. She accepted that about her sister; Mary had other plans. When she heard that Danny had not asked for Sophie's hand—her father nearby or no—she decided he was a trifling, deceitful, deceiving man who didn't deserve an O'Faolain for a wife. The tempering thought they all lived in dangerous times lasted the blink of an eye.

Sophia stood and left the table with a stiff: "Good night, then, *Mister* Kavanagh. We'll be off in the morning. Perhaps you could find a nun in this pagan city to teach you how to write a proper letter. I believe you should explain yourself." Mary shot him an imperious look and marched out the door with her sister.

"Look, Jim, it's like this. I know I can trust your discretion, but I'm not going to risk your safety by telling you any more than you need to know. Let's just say I've volunteered for a very special, very risky IRB mission. After the Devlin business, I convinced myself that I didn't have the heart for any more of it. Living here the last while, though, has really opened my eyes to what needs to be done, must be done. We're surrounded by spies, informers, traitors of our own kind. There are hundreds of Devlins in this town, each one worse than the one before. We'll never be free with them against us, Tommies or no, police or no, Lewis guns or no. These people must be—um—made ineffective. That's my job, along with some others.

"Now maybe you can see my problem. What good would a dead husband be to her, then? Or, worse, one in prison for the rest of his life, and her with my name on her back? Or one who has so much blood on his hands he can't live with himself—or anyone else? I'm not saying I'm backing out. I'm not. It has to be done. I'm just one man, but if I can do something to set this country free, then, by God, I will. Listen to me. I sound like Padraig Pearse.

"Anyway, these things are spinning around in my head and driving me crazy. I told her I loved her—just happened, slipped out—probably shouldn't have—but I can't bring myself to ask her to marry me. Not now, at least. And I don't know how to explain it all to her. I thought that maybe, if we could talk, you could give me some help on this. I'd rather cut off my arm than see her like she was tonight. That's the God's honest truth. There, I'm done."

Jim Murtagh sat with his head bowed while Danny spoke. He could see no end of trouble for these two, especially after what he heard in Dundalk. He sipped his drink and considered for a few minutes. Danny began to speak, but Murtagh raised his hand to silence him, looking him in the eye as a friend, not a priest.

"First of all, Danny, I think you underestimate her. She's quite aware that the situation this country is in requires hardship and sacrifice. Your gentlemanly reticence, if you'll forgive me, is outmoded and doesn't sound quite right coming from the mouth of a bogtrotting Fenian renegade. She's for you; you're for her. You both come from the same blood. I know this sure as I'm sitting here. Your life will be lost if you don't take her. So will hers. I'll not mention your soul. There. That part's over.

"As to your situation right now, I have to agree with you. Marriage would not be wise, and it might put her at risk. No, no, don't say anything. I'll explain in a minute. However, I do not agree with you keeping your mouth shut. What are your orders tomorrow?"

"I'm to report at 8:30 for training near St. Brendan's Hospital."

"Right. Sophia and I are going to 6:00 Mass. The train leaves Sackville Street station at 7:30. You be on the platform at 7:00. Don't have any second thoughts about this, just do it. I will have a long talk with Sophia, and I think I can make her understand your dilemma and the reason for your idiotic, thick-headed silence. Really, Danny, you should have gone to the Jesuits and learned some logic. I'll be as plain as I can: Ask her to marry you, not right now, not even next year, but make it clear that in a better world you would do it tomorrow. Rely on her good sense, her love for you, for Ireland, and, for God's sake, her intelligence. Just listen to me, sounding like a Jesuit meself. I mean all this as a friend, Danny. It's advice, of course, but I think it's sound."

It was Danny Kavanagh's turn to sit in silence, pondering. Jim Murtagh knew he had to tell him sooner, rather than later.

"Thanks. You're a wise man. I think what you say is right, so I'll do it. God help me—and her—but I'll do it. It's a relief, that's for sure. Couldn't find my way out. Felt like I was in a box with dirt being shoveled on it."

"That's grand, Danny. No one can ever be sure in this life, but I think you're doing right. The one thing I've never seen Sophia O'Faolain do is let go of something or somebody she loves. Put your faith in that—what faith you have, I mean."

"Ah, guess I deserved that."

"We'll just have one more small taste of the Irish, Danny. There's something I've got to tell you."

Over their last drink, Jim Murtagh told Danny Kavanagh that the Devlin family had found out who shot Eddie Devlin in the back of the head and pushed his body into the River Fane. "You'll not be surprised, Danny, that these lads say they don't believe Eddie informed on you and your brother; they say you robbed and murdered him; they don't give a straw for what the IRB or the IRA have to say, either.

"They're a feuding, wicked bunch, in my opinion; not very bright, not very loyal to anyone but themselves and the main chance; cowardly, through and through. Even so, never underestimate the deviousness of cowardice. What I heard in Dundalk is they have sworn revenge, blood for blood, so I'd be extra careful if I were you. Not that you need more problems right now. The only good thing is that the IRB has shut them out, and they don't know where you are, and they have no idea Sophia was involved, far as I can tell. They've tried checking around in Crossmaglen, of course, but they're terrified of Mick and the brigade. They wouldn't dare take him on at home, not that they're after him, I hope, but I did take the precaution of warning him."

He stood very still, watching her, memorizing her for the empty time to come. The white light pouring through the station's glass roof fell on her soft, like the gentle cascade of angels' wings. The rest: crowd noise, hiss of locomotive steam, people breaking by him in waves, were unreal, silent: out of focus, stage props, unimportant, flat. She was facing away from him, standing by herself on the platform. Erect, watching tense, swelling graceful in outline, wearing a long, brown linen skirt and a matching jacket that hugged her waist.

Her knitted cloche hat was of the same color, with a wide band of black satin above the narrow brim. In her right hand she held a black umbrella; the other was closed in a fist.

Danny walked to her and put his hand on her shoulder. She spun to him, collapsing against him, winding her arms around him in an embrace so tight, so close, so intense, that passersby stared in shock at such a physical and public display, more so when they saw the priest in the compartment window staring straight ahead with a smile on his face. Such things just weren't done in Catholic Dublin, 1918. Everyone had a better sense of decorum—or maybe shame.

He kissed her on the lips; she kissed him on the lips. Two more things that just weren't done. Like children, they held each other, cheek to cheek, and, like a child, she said: "Whatever it is, whatever you have to do, you must do, you have to do, just don't leave me—ever. We will wait until it's time. I will keep you safe."

In turn, he said, like a child, "I can't, ever. No matter where I am, what I've done, I will never leave you. You are my wife, Sophia O'Faolain. One day, it will be over, then it will be the way it should be. Always: if I can't find you, you must find me. Promise."

"I will always find you, always be with you, no matter what. 'Till time and times are done,' my love. 'Till time and times are done.'" Then her forehead was against his chest, beside it her clenched fist. He took her hand; it opened, and into his she dropped a slender golden chain and a wafer thin locket. He held it tight in the block of his fist. In a blur, the conductor called, the hiss of steam rose to a pulse, and she was gone. He felt a bayonet go through his gut; it bent him over. She did not look back. He had nothing to give her, except his life. He could not die; he could not be caught; he must survive; must.

Michael Collins was far too busy with all the details of the secret war, his position in the newly elected government, his coordination of the IRA brigades, the logistics, the training, the endless meetings, the unacknowledged and very secret activities of the Irish Republican Brotherhood that stood beneath the IRA like a granite shelf. To lighten the load, he delegated Liam Tobin and Tom Cullen to run the Twelve Apostles; still under his ultimate direction, of course. Tobin began the brief meeting in the cramped Antient Concert Room on Brunswick Street:

"Right, Charlie, Danny, yer man is one Detective Gallagher. He's the charming individual sent in from Tipperary to identify our commanders from there when they come to the city. We're quite sure of him, one of the Igoe Gang, the traitors. You'll remember Bill Redmond? He's never come out of Dublin Castle, never will, and we're quite certain Gallagher is responsible. Harry Duffy here will go with you and point him out. He'll be just finishing his liquid meal at the Stag's Head on Dame Street."

As they walked toward the pub, young Charlie Dolan was clearly nervous: "Christ, Danny, I just don't know. I've never done anything like this before. Have you?"

"Take a deep breath, Charlie. You can do it. Once he's pointed out, I'll come in from the front; you come in from the side. Don't forget: shoot, drop yer arm and walk away. Just like we trained. I'll finish it if it comes to that."

"Jaysus, Mary and Joseph, yer a hard one, that's sure."

"Right, we're on. Duffy just raised his hat to the big one in the brown suit."

Detective Gallagher turned and watched the man who greeted him walk away and disappear into the crowd on the street. "Now what the hell was that about?" he thought. "No one I know, that's certain. I'll check on that bird later." As he turned back, he came face to face with Danny Kavanagh, nodded his head and tried to step around him. From the corner of his eye, he could see Charlie Dolan quickly coming at him from his left. Danny raised the Webley and fired a round directly into the detective's chest. The pistol kicked, and he heard the heavy smack of the large bullet. The body crumpled where it stood, a heap of clothes and meat on the black stone pavement. Charlie Dolan bent over the body, watching the blood spreading like porter. He pointed his small automatic at the side of the head, glanced at Danny for an instant, fear on his face, then pulled the trigger. Danny took a quick look, ready to fire again, but it wasn't necessary. The crowd had scattered after the first shot. They couldn't take their eyes off the corpse or the blood. Danny Kavanagh and Charlie Dolan walked away and disappeared down Crow Lane.

"Christ have mercy, Danny, that was one ugly thing we did back there. So much blood in a man. Didn't know the bullets made such big holes coming out. Hope we got the right man. Jaysus." The two men were walking too quickly along Arran

Quay, on the north side of the Liffey, when Dolan stopped short to talk.

"Charlie, that's none of our affair. Tobin and Cullen know. The Big Fella knows. That's enough. Come on, keep moving. We're not outta this yet. Now what?"

"I'll just step into the church here and say a small prayer for the man. Coming? It's only right."

"No time for that. I'll see you in Brunswick Street in one hour. We've more to do."

And they did have more to do, much more. It was the first of many shootings by the Twelve Apostles, by Danny Kavanagh. He became even more cold, deliberate, pitiless, shooting without the slightest hesitation or remorse. Slowly, the eyes of the Castle were being closed, two by two. As the secret war between the IRA and the police became a public war that involved the British garrison, as the spies and police were silenced, as the flying columns had one success after another, the rage of impotence rose in the gorge of Westminster across the Irish Sea. The ranks of the Royal Irish Constabulary were thinning, by death, by resignation, by fear. In response, the British government let loose first the Black and Tans, then the Auxiliaries. Their power was absolute, their exploits notorious, their cruelty legendary. They were not the police, not the army, but something else: the dogs of war.

Danny Kavanagh considered all of it. As far as he was concerned he was a soldier under orders from an army duly formed by the democratically elected government in the *Dail*. Eamon de Valera was the president. Even though he was in America raising money and support, he knew everything. Danny's job was to eliminate the enemies of his country in time of war, but what were the Tans, the Auxies? Those out-of-work Great War veterans burned houses, looted, killed civilians, even priests, enraged that the flying columns in the country couldn't be found, the Twelve Apostles vanished into Dublin crowds, Michael Collins was nowhere and everywhere. Hate hardened in Danny Kavanagh's soul. He hadn't seen Collins, or Mulcahy, or McKee for many months. It didn't matter. He knew he was doing right. He hoped he was doing right.

The private war became very public on December 7, 1919, when Liam Lynch loosed his flying column against a detachment of the King's Shropshire Light Infantry on their way to church in County Cork. The reprisals against civilians started quickly. The smoking bodies of the Irish Igoe Gang piled up on Dublin streets. Thanks to friends in Dublin Castle, and his own outrageous daring, by fall, 1920, Michael Collins had collected all the details he needed about his main adversary: the Cairo Gang. The strategy for this group of British intelligence officers was straightforward: break the Collins organization and assassinate Sinn Fein members of the government, even though they were not involved in the military. The time had almost come to strike at the Hydra's head.

1 February 1920,
Dublin

My dearest Sophia,

   It's been a few weeks, I know, but things are hard here, and sometimes it's difficult to find time to sit down and write a *proper* letter, as you would call it.

We have to move around a lot. I understand what you say about my letters being all stiff and formal. It's that nun's fault you wanted me to hire. So I'll try just to write like I speak. Don't blame me if the grammar ain't right.

My job has more to do than ever, it feels like. But it's become easier over time. The boss got the inside track on some of our competition last April, and we're planning to beat them at their own game shortly. They're imports from overseas—the Middle East, they say—and they're not playing fair at all in our business.

Sometimes, when there's a break, I walk over to St. Stephen's Green, sit at our spot by the pond and think. Remember, really. I don't want to forget your face at the train station that day. The sound of your voice. The color of your eyes. Don't worry, I haven't lost your locket with your photograph in it. It goes everywhere I go. It's just that I'm tired. At night, when I can't sleep, I wonder whether it's all worth it. Will it work this time? I wonder where you are, what you're doing, thinking. I want you happy. I miss you.

The place I'm staying at right now isn't so bad, but there are a lot of stairs to climb. You think so, I know, but Dublin doesn't really smell all that bad, except when the tide is out. Then the Liffey is a terror, especially with the warmer weather coming on soon. I'd rather the honest smell of our farm in Crossmaglen. Cleaner, I guess. The hills and glens there beat Grafton Street any day. Not sure about Tourmakeady.

The team has moved to new, bigger premises that we set up as a painter's and decorator's office. I enjoyed that, building the counters, the cupboards and all. Just like it used to be when I was in Armagh. Like I said before, there's something about the smell of wood and the shavings the plane makes. I'm the building expert on staff.

All right, I can hear you saying too much stiff and formal. I love you. I want to be with you. I want to marry you, now, today. I want out, over, done. When the job is finished, everything will be as one again. The way it should be. I miss you.

Charlie, the young lad I told you about, is coming on fine. He'll be turning 18 in a week or two. Please tell Mary I'm not such a bad sort. Regards to your father. Hope he's keeping up with his duties. Jim Murtagh knows what I think already.

Your loving Husband,
Danny

"Thank you kindly, Mrs. Dolan, but I've had about as much tea as I can hold. Your cakes are very good, indeed." She quickly passed him the plate—again. "Ah, grand, thanks. Where's the birthday boy? He's behind his time."

"He'll be back shortly, I hope. Perhaps he stopped to chat after Mass. He's such a devout boy, don't you think, Mr. Kavanagh? Never misses an opportunity to take the sacrament, and such a one for his devotion to the Virgin Mary and the rosary. Even more so of late. I'm so proud of him, now that he's working for the government, and him so young yet. It's a lot of responsibility. Charlie's told me a lot about you, Mr. Kavanagh. You're an Armagh man, aren't you? He did mention it, but I can hear it in your voice. So refreshing, like a trip to the country. Do you work with my boy all the time in the accounting department?"

Danny Kavanagh sat stiffly, on the edge of an upholstered chair in the Dolan's ornate and costly parlor, trying to balance the impossibly delicate plate and tea cup on his knees. He was terrified of breaking something or spilling tea on the wine red and cream turkey carpet under the feet he knew for a certainty were far too big. He was wearing the best civilian clothes he had, but not those Charlie Dolan had given him that had belonged to his dead father. His uniform—made for him by Tom Cullen's tailor—was too dangerous to wear on the street. For the occasion, he had left the Webley behind, but a small, 25 caliber Walther automatic was strapped to his calf. Charlie's mother was the complete picture of the wealthy Dublin widow: well dressed to the neck of her ice white, lacy bodice, strings of pearls, a cameo brooch, her ringed hands handling the silver tea service with the meticulous grace of long practice. She was gracious and lovely at forty. Apparently, she did not see his scar, looking him frankly in the eyes.

"Well, actually no, Mrs. Dolan. Charlie and I only work together sometimes, on special projects. We're part of a team, see, so we have to do what our team leaders tell us to. But we work well together—when we do I mean. Charlie's a good lad, just needs a bit more experience is all. Did I hear his dainty foot at the door?"

Charlie Dolan, fresh from communion, rushed into the room and straight to his mother. She stood, quickly, took him in her arms, kissed his cheek, and, cooing, smoothed his hair again and again. "Here's my baby back, Mr. Kavanagh. He's such a good boy, almost a man."

Tom Cullen looked up from the paper spread on his desk. "Danny, the Big Fella says you should take this one. Something about 'a debt to pay.' There are two, an Irishman by the name of Billy O'Neill and his keeper, a big Englishman by the name of...let me see...Smythe."

"Right, Tom, I know those two well enough. Saw more than I'd like of them around the Castle. No need for someone to point them out. Not necessary, not worth the risk."

"Who do you want to go with you?"

"I think Charlie Dolan's the man, sir."

"Sure, are you? Your report after the Gallagher business said he was a bit hesitant. Can't have that. The big Brit hoor is no pushover. What with all his people that haven't come back, he'll be right on his guard. Word is he's almost as good a shot as you are. You'll have to be damned careful."

"And so I will, Tom, and so I will. No, Charlie's up to it. We'll need a few days to find the right place and the right time."

"Fine, but the schedule I've been given says no more that a week. Could get in the way of the big show, later. This file's not complete yet. Send Charlie round for it tomorrow."

"That's plenty of time, Tom, plenty of time."

"The kips? Now, then, my dapper young man who lives with his mother in the fine north of Dublin, what would you be knowin about the kips over in Nighttown? Stealin down after Mass for a roll with some of the girls, eh? I'm shocked, truly I am. Would it be one at a time, or two? Three? Saints above."

"Danny, don't say such a thing. If my mother ever heard...." Charlie Dolan blessed himself quickly. "I'd never...

I've never... I've read the file, is all. They're regulars, those
boys. Every Saturday night they go from around the Castle
over to Bella Cohen's old place on Tyrone, behind the
Custom House. Usually come out around 1. That'll be the
time. Drunk as lords, all satisfied with themselves."

"Ah, that's a good man, yerself. Thanks for the directions.
Now yer talkin about satisfaction like a seasoned veteran. I
knew there was more to yez than the clothes."

Charlie blushed deeply. "Give it a rest, Danny. It'll be the
best time."

"Yer right, young Dolan. Nighttown it'll be. But look sharp,
Charlie, the Brit's a tough old cock. O'Neill will be easy, but
not the other. Don't look, don't think, just shoot. Got it?"

"Got it."

Despite the bravado, Danny Kavanagh hadn't been
anywhere near the Dublin kips since he'd been in the city. It
wasn't modesty, or fear, or religion that kept him out of the
brothels. It was loyalty to Sophia O'Faolain, pure and simple.
When he scouted the filthy streets around Bella Cohen's by
himself, he thought he was back in the alleys in 1916 when he
and his brother, Mick, got out of the GPO on the Trusty
Triumph.

Day and night, the kennels ran with sewage; men, women, children, everyone, drunk, sick, hopeless, selling whatever they had, themselves included, for just one more drink. The slit trench alleys, garbage strewn, rank with decaying food, animals, people. The overwhelming smells were chamber pots emptied out the windows and sodden, unwashed woolen clothes. The damp rose up the walls, the legs, the hearts, the souls of the inmates. It was Bedlam without guards. Block upon block moaned with insanity, thirst, grief, pleasure. The begging shawlies and their filthy broods jostled for position with the younger whores in their cheap dresses and smeared make-up. Soldiers and sailors took their pick, standing them up against the slick, grimy brick or kneeling them down for a few minutes of heaven.

They got there at 12:30 on the night of the operation. Charlie Dolan told his mother he was going to the novena, then midnight mass.

"Howya, there, big man. Who's your little boy? Yer son? Out to break him in, are yez? Come here to Molly, lover boy, I'll teach yez all yez need to know."

"Bugger off. Let the lad be."

"Oh, so it's bugger, is it? Didn't think you fancied the ladies when I set eyes on yez, ye dirty pervert." She hawked and spat noisily on the pavement before turning to her next prospect. They did make an odd pair: Danny in his beggar's clothes, Charlie not as well dressed as usual, but well enough. He couldn't help it.

"Holy Mary, Danny, was this my idea? What a dog's breakfast this place is."

"It was, ye dirty pervert. Hurry up; we'll be behind our time. Keep yer eyes to the front, there's a good lad. The wee girl's just relievin herself, is all."

The rain beat in sheets. The kennels ran, rife with bobbing souls washing toward the Liffey. Bella Cohen's was once a fairly grand house, with a decent brick front, not too dirty. The steps had been swept and the door painted within living memory. Bright squares of light shone from the windows on all three floors; even above the hammering rain, they could hear the piano, the laughter, the squeals of false delight. Two doors away stood St. Mary's Penitent Retreat, a home for reformed whores.

Danny and Charlie took refuge from the rain and prying eyes in a crack of a laneway across the street. "Okay,

Charlie, like I said, I'll set up shop just outside the door. If O'Neill's not too drunk, he'll probably recognize old 'Bootface' and stop for a word. Smythe, the shitbreeches, will wade in for a go at me. That's when you come up behind. I'll get the first one I can; you try for the other. Remember, just shoot, don't think. We'll get em, alright. No lie, son. No lie."

Some men are affable and kind after a night in the pubs, the kips. Some become increasingly angry, cruel. O'Neill and Smythe perfectly illustrated the two ends of the scale when they poured from the brothel. "Fucking Dublin, pissing down as always," Smythe said as he opened his umbrella. "Ah, no. It's just a wee mist, is all. We don't get rain in Dublin. Lots of floods, but no rain to speak of," from O'Neill as he, too, raised his umbrella to the thumping rain. "Let's find us a cab, boyo. Well now, wouldya just look here, Jim. Bootface risen from the dead. What happened to ye, old son? The lads at the Castle thought you made the last ride to Glasnevin—or the Liffey. Here's a bit for a drink."

Smythe pushed O'Neill aside, knocking the coin from his hand. "I told you last time, you fucking arselicking sod, to make yourself scarce. Apparently, you're too much the stupid Papist Mick to get that through your thick head, so I will personally see that you do." Smythe took the revolver from under his arm, holding the barrel in his hand, preparing the use the butt on Danny Kavanagh's head. He sensed movement behind him, and just as quickly the butt was in his palm. "So, that's your game, is it? Irish scum."

Billy O'Neill stepped in front of the big man. "Hold on, now Jim, there's a good lad. Old Bootface here wouldn't hurt a nun, would ye now, boyo?" He bent down to Danny, weaving and smiling as he said it. Danny lifted his head and looked O'Neill right in the eye. O'Neill saw for the first time the young, green-eyed mask of death. He stood bolt upright, and all he managed to get out was "Here, now, what's...," before Danny shot him twice in the face. Charlie Dolan was still too far away, but he opened fire on the Englishman. Smythe held the dying Billy O'Neill in front of him, so Danny couldn't get a shot, and banged off two rounds in Charlie's direction. Then he pushed the body on top of Danny, knocking the pistol from his hand. Smythe smiled, kicked it clattering away into the rain, pumped two more shots into the heap on the ground, and turned for young Charlie Dolan.

O'Neill's blood was running into Danny's eyes. One of Smythe's shots had hit him in the lower leg. He hoped

Charlie had the good sense to retreat. He heard more shots, but could see nothing. Two were from Smythe's heavy revolver; two were from a small automatic like the one Charlie carried. One, he could not identify. Danny reached down, felt the hole in his calf and pulled the Walther from its holster.

He could hear Smythe shouting, "Fine shot, lad." Then the big Englishman pulled O'Neill's body away. His look was that of a grinning demon from some screaming circle of Dante's hell. "Now for you, Paddy." Danny Kavanagh emptied the automatic into his chest, and Smythe roared in a fury that turned to agony as his heart burst.

Danny crawled for the Webley, wondering how many shells were still in the chambers. He hoisted his back against the dripping brick. In the middle of the road, Charlie Dalton's well dressed body smoked in an awkward pile, knees on the street, forehead on the cobbles. A man stepped from the doorway of St. Mary's Penitent Retreat carrying what looked like a Mauser rifle-pistol, like the one the Countess used in 1916. He was wary, advancing slowly. Danny Kavanagh waited as long as he could, trying to clear the blood and rain from his eyes, then fired. The first shot shattered the brick near the man's head; the second hit him in the left hand. The man dropped to his knees and got off two wild rounds before scuttling off into the darkness.

"Jaysus, what can I say to his mother?" Danny thought. He was absolutely certain Charlie Dolan was dead.

One week later, Collins, Mulcahy and McKee sat in an upstairs room of Vaughan's Hotel, papers and glasses spread out before them. There was a knock on the door, and Christy Hart, the ancient porter, looked in. "Sorry, surs, but there's a gentleman here wants a word with yez." Danny Kavanagh pushed by him, hobbled to the table and rested his weight on his two fists.

"Sorry for the interruption. What's the story? I've waited and waited. I need to know, now. Who is he? Where? He's mine, that one. Where's the famous security now? We should have been warned they had a shadow."

Mulcahy consulted his watch; McKee looked at Danny with a mixture of irritation and sympathy. He'd been to the Dolan funeral as well; it was dangerous, but he decided to go with Liam Tobin. McKee had been to many funerals, but he'd never seen grief like that before. He saw Danny Kavanagh's face dissolve in anguish when the mother said, "Mr. Kavanagh, I hold you personally responsible for this. He was just a baby, my only baby, and you killed him. Hate does not describe what I feel for you."

Michael Collins smoothed the hair from his eyes. His look was somber, stern; fine, square jaw set. "Danny, there was no possible way we could have known about him. I was going to talk to you later. Just found out last night. You have to understand that we've been a bit busy planning for Sunday's festivities. I understand how you feel about young Dolan, we all share that, but casualties are inevitable, unfortunate, but inevitable. The man who got him had nothing to do with the Castle or the Cairo Gang of spies, either. His name is Peter Devlin, brother to one Eddie Devlin of Inniskeen. It was you he was after, Danny, not Charlie Dolan, rest him."

Danny Kavanagh's face turned once more to the young mask of death. "Right. Where is he now? He won't be breathing long, the bastard."

Collins raised his slender hand. "Now, Danny, calm down, there's a good lad. Peter Devlin won't be needing his return ticket north. Liam Tobin sent two of the squad after him this morning. They found him in Sandymount. It will be called a disappearance. There will be nothing to tie it to you."

"Fine, I'll be off to Inniskeen then. I'll wipe out the whole nest of those dogs. You and I know they'll just keep on coming."

Mulcahy stood up quickly, imperious, angry: "Lieutenant Kavanagh, you forget yourself. We'll have no personal vendettas here. None. That's final. Sit down. You, sir, will learn to follow orders if I have to teach you myself, personally." He traced a whole series of invisible Xs in the air as he spoke.

Danny sat stiffly, his bandaged leg straight out in front of him. Michael Collins glanced at Mulcahy, who sank heavily to his chair. Collins said, "Danny, look, we've taken as many precautions as we can. I sent a wire to Matt O'Faolain this afternoon. Sophia is well protected, trust me. Father Murtagh will know by now. So will your brother in Crossmaglen. When there's time, I will personally have a word with these Devlins of Inniskeen. This business stops now, or I will stop them. And, sorry to say, I will stop you as well. What we're doing is far, far too important to be jeopardized by something like this."

"Sorry, Mick, I apologize to all of you, but I can't shake the sound of Mrs. Dolan's voice at the grave. And I have to know that Sophia's absolutely safe. I'll need a few days up there. You have my word I won't go anywhere near Inniskeen. I'll be back, sure, before Sunday."

"Sorry, Danny, can't allow it. Maybe later. You're simply too important to the plan to risk. I would if I could, but I can't. You'll excuse us now? There's a good lad." Impatient, Collins turned to McKee: "Now Dick, really, as far as Dev is concerned we've got enough of the negotiating sort, so I don't think we can trust...." His head snapped around quickly when McKee's brows shot up. "Kavanagh, you're dismissed."

On Sunday morning, November 21, 1920, Michael Collins cut off the Hydra's head. He thought it was permanent. The killing started at 9:00, precisely. Mulcahy demanded that, and the Big Fella agreed. Danny Kavanagh was the only one of the Twelve Apostles among the fourteen men assigned to Pembroke Street, the secret headquarters of the Cairo Gang of British agents. The rest of his squad was scattered around the city, assigned to get different men and make sure the job was done right.

Paddy Flanagan, a Captain in C Company of Dublin No. 2 Brigade, and Danny were the senior members of the group. They knocked politely at the front door, waited inside for the clock to strike the hour and began. Some of the agents were shot in bed, some in their doorways, some on the landing leading to the rooms. Paddy and Danny were methodical, practised, quick, accurate. The stairs were running with blood. The youngest of the killing team, seventeen-year-old Archie Griffin, was told to guard four agents at the bottom of the stairs. Blood trickling around his feet, Archie's face was ashen, bottom lip quivering, revolver shaking in his hand. The four agents thought they had a chance to escape. From the landing above, Danny looked down and knew what to do.

"Right, Paddy, let's get it over." Paddy Flanagan elbowed the crying Archie Griffin out of the way. Together, they herded the men into the basement. Danny asked the names of two of them and checked them off the list after Paddy shot them in the temple. In turn, Danny did the shooting and Paddy checked off the names.

All over Dublin, the shots rang out as the church bells tolled the hour. It was all over by 9:30. Fourteen members of the Cairo Gang died; two more than the civilians the Black and Tans shot at Croke Park later in the day. The score was more than evened when Dick McKee, Commandant of the Dublin Brigade, the man with the Pied Piper voice, and Pedar Clancy had their fingernails pulled out before they were bayoneted and shot through the head in the cells of Dublin Castle. The Black and Tans went berserk in the streets of Dublin.

23 December 1920,
Dublin

My dearest Sophia,

This one has to be short. No time. Happy Christmas, my love. I'm sad not to be with you, especially now.

It's not fair at all, but I'm not to be allowed to see you. Once everything was sorted out on the Sunday, I thought I'd get some time off. The answer is no. I think they don't want me anywhere near Inniskeen. Later on, I'm to move south to join up with the lads in Cork, a kind of goodwill ambassador from Dublin. There is no possible way you should consider coming down here. It's not safe. We'll just have to think about the spring. I'm moving further away, but I'm closer to you than ever. Trust in that. It does look like the job might be working after all. The company from overseas seems to be having some second thoughts about the investment here.

Please give my best wishes for the season to everyone, especially Jim Murtagh. He'll be busy, no doubt, blessing every goose in Dundalk. Of course, I'd rather the Christmas deer in Crossmaglen with you by me.

Don't fret. I healed up fine after my accident. Young Charlie is especially in my mind just now. The only thing that makes all this possible is you.

Your loving Husband,
Danny

PART III

———————————————————

GREEN AGAINST GREEN

7. "Glory O"

14 July 1921,
Dundalk

My Dearest Danny,

I didn't tell you in any of my letters, but by the time spring was over, I was fit to be tied. I wanted to write Michael Collins himself and give him a large piece of my mind. My father forbade it. Orders, says he, are orders. Orders or no, it's been far too long since you've been here with me. Every soldier, no matter how important, deserves leave, and it's cruel you haven't had any these long years. And it's been terribly hard on me. I understand the reasons well enough, but this has nothing to do with my brain. You know what I mean.

But now, now, surely you'll be coming back north. The news of the truce is wonderful, even Father Murtagh seems to think so. Please write as soon as you can and tell me when you'll come. I'm tired of waiting, tired of not seeing you, not hearing your voice.

You are my husband, and I want you home safe, here, with me, no matter what the IRA or the IRB have to say. It's only right after all you've been through.

Now, just as surely, the war is over and we've won. Everything you've fought for, everything we've sacrificed, it's all been for the good. The papers say Dublin is quiet these days, so if there's any delay at all, I'll be on the next train to you. Let me know, my love, let me know soonest.

As always, I pray for your safety.

Your loving Wife,
Sophia

"What the hell is GHQ on about, anyway? I didn't get any notice about this. Who the hell are you?"

"Here are my orders, sir. They said the Big Fella himself issued them. Funny they didn't tell you in advance."

Liam Lynch stood abruptly from his desk and swiped them out of Danny's hand with a snort and a frustrated roundhouse. A thin, sharp-faced man nearing thirty, with a quickly receding, sandy hairline, he read quietly for a few minutes, the papers between the hands that supported him on the desk top. He finally raised his head to look directly at Danny, not sparing the new man an inspection of his scar.

"Even before I read all this, I was pretty much aware, Lieutenant Kavanagh, of who you are, where you're from and how you got that scar. You're a long way from home. They'll be a lot of the men here who'll be lookin up to a hero of the GPO, no doubt. However, so far as I'm concerned, you're here under protest. I requested trained, seasoned officers for field operations, not some back alley gunman, not some eyes and ears from the city. You're IRB, aren't you? That's one good thing at least."

"I am. Beggin your pardon, sir, I did what I was ordered to do, just like you. There'll be a lot fewer losses of our field commanders now, when they come up to Dublin. I've no orders to report to anybody in the city. I was told I'm here to help out, any way I can. I'm ready for that, sir."

Lynch sat back down and perched his chin on his right fist. With the fingers of his other hand, he scrubbed his thinning hair, then rubbed the red-rimmed eyes. "Well, perhaps, Kavanagh. Maybe you don't know that way down here in County Cork we're desperately short of arms and ammunition. While you lot have been shooting up the town at will, we've had to curtail our operations. I've told Collins that a thousand times; Mulcahy as well. Why don't we get supplies instead of excuses? It's like we're talking to a Dublin backhouse. Shite.

"Your file here says you're a damned good shot, rifle or pistol. That's just wonderful. Some of our men could certainly use instruction, but what the hell good are you if we have nothing to shoot? For Christ's sake, man, I've got 300 Lee-Enfields and 140 pistols. Probably have about one round for each weapon. What are we supposed to do?"

"Excuse me, sir, but I thought a truce was on?"

"What? You don't swallow that Brit horseshite, do ye? Lloyd George is probably just taking time to develop a new offensive, get his spies back in. As for Collins, it's anyone's guess what he's up to."

Danny had tried to maintain his composure in the face of this onslaught from a man he had only heard about: Liam Lynch, the flying column commander who had given the British Army almost as many losses as Tom Barry during the public war that had been suspended since the 11th of July. When Collins didn't get the respect Danny thought was due, he decided to wade in: "Hold on a minute. I've worked with Mick Collins close, like, since '17. I'd like to know what you meant by that last bit...sir. After all, Mick and all the GHQ are under the direct command of the Dail and President de Valera, now he's back from the States."

"Oh, please, spare me. A babe in the woods with a pistol in his hand. Really, Kavanagh, where have you been? Dev has no power—none—over the army. Got that? He wasn't around for the fighting, so what IRA man in his right mind will listen to him about this so-called truce? Besides, he's not much of a soldier. You, of all people, should know that. He's even turned his back on us, on the IRB. Nobody down here seems to know what this cease fire is about, or why Dev signed Lloyd George's terms, and we get damned little information from the city. I have no time for a truce King George wanted. Far as I'm concerned, it was the Brits needing time to regroup, so we're still at war down here."

Before he got to County Cork, Danny saw the truce as relief, rest, an end to the killing. Listening to one of the most important military commanders in Ireland made him much less certain—less relieved. "If that's your orders, sir, I'm bound to follow, though I can't agree with you—entirely. Seems to me that I might help out by finding some ammunition hereabouts. I'd like to remind you that I'm a country man, from County Armagh. Up there, we don't let small things like ownership get in the way."

2 August 1921,
Strabane, Co. Tyrone

Dear Pagan,

Even though we might not have to be so careful of what we say in letters any more, I'll have this one forwarded to you through church channels. It will be difficult to write, but I'll just press on. I'm sorry to say I've lost quite a bit of the enthusiasm I had for the truce last month. I'm a northern man, you're a northern man, so I'll speak plainly. The situation in Ulster is a bloodbath in the making. Once the English set up the parliament in Belfast, I knew things would get much, much worse. No matter what happens with the truce, it's plain that some or all of Ulster will remain in English hands. With Craig in power there, backed up by that bigot Carson, they'll be no hope for Catholic people, Irish people. None. And I count you among them.

I don't think Collins or Mulcahy believe they can win a protracted war with the English over the issue. Sensible, that; the British Empire is a mighty foe. But it shouldn't mean we should agree to a divided country. We hold the strongest position we've had in centuries, and it would be foolish to let go our advantage. I'm no great admirer of President de Valera—he did sign the truce, after all—but I read in The Irish Times he said publicly, "An Ireland fragmented nobody cares about." I'd have to agree with him there, if he means it. Division would mean the border country—including your beloved Crossmaglen—would be burning forever. I've talked to Mick, and your brother seems to be of much the same mind. He's a more patient man than you are, though, and he says he'll bide his time, keep his people in reserve.

I thought it fair to say all this. Your letters tell me you're preoccupied with Dublin and its concerns. I don't want to be too pessimistic, but de Valera, Collins, Mulcahy, the lot, should be making much more noise about Ulster than they are. In the south, it seems everyone is just happy to have a truce. In the north, they've let loose a bunch of criminals called the B-Specials. Just think of the Tans and the Auxies in different uniforms. What they're doing is not pretty, and there's no one to stop them. Mick didn't say, but I think the IRA here has been told to stand down for the time being.

Last week, I went to Inniskeen to try to resolve the situation. No luck, I'm afraid. Rather the opposite. The remaining Devlins are just as bent on revenge as Peter was. And there's a lot of them. They seem not to care that he shot Charlie Dolan, and they don't believe for a minute that he simply disappeared. I think the Devlins might have links to the Specials. I'd have a care if I were you.

Enough. Sophia is blooming, waiting for your return on leave. Perhaps I could bend a few rules on the publishing of the banns and whatnot, so you two could get married quite quickly. Do give me some notice, though, my friend. Because of the way things are here—and not only with the Devlins—we should keep the ceremony private and quiet—well, quiet as we can with your lot.

Whether you like it or not, you are in my prayers.

Yours in Christ,
Jim Murtagh

1 September 1921,
Mitchelstown, Co. Cork

Dear Jim,

Your letter finally caught up with me. Right now, I couldn't be further away from Dublin. I read the papers, like you do, and I can't understand either what's going on with Ulster. What I do I don't like. Seems to me that we fought for all of Ireland, not just the south. I can't live with the idea of Crossmaglen, or Armagh, Strabane, or Belfast, for that matter, belonging to the Brits. That's not why I did what I had to do. That's not why I put my life on hold like this.

It's all getting very confusing down here. Nobody seems to know who's in charge—outside the brigade, that is. When I was in Dublin, I had no idea that the army in the field had any problems at all with GHQ. Here, it's all resentment and mistrust. De Valera isn't regarded that highly, and neither is the Big Fella. They're much more interested in Cathal Brugha and Rory O'Connor. Some of the lads think they're the men to lead us out of the truce mess with a clear victory. Most of them think as I do, that the English have to leave, all of them, from every place. That's the only kind of truce or peace I want.

I'm holding back replying to Sophia's last letter until this has time to reach you. She'll be furious and heartbroken at the same time that I can't come to her. You already know how I feel. Liam Lynch says there's no chance for a while yet. He's a hard man, but a good commander, and I've come to trust his judgment. After all, he's the one who surrounded the Brits with flying columns.

I'm in an odd position here. Before, I thought I knew everything that was going on in Dublin. Seems I didn't. Now, I don't know anything.

You've been a true friend. Please help me by helping Sophia when she gets my letter. I'll try to keep doing my duty as best I can.

Pagan, indeed!

In friendship,
Danny

7 September 1921,
Mitchelstown, Co. Cork

My dearest Sophia,

Your letter didn't find me until just a short while ago. I wrote you it might happen, and I've been transferred down here by army order. My new commandant seems a good fellow, and I've lots of new duties to carry out. It's no good. I just don't know what to say. It's not my fault. Everything's so confusing and messed about. On top of all that, I can't understand why I'm not allowed leave. Is it the Big Fella or my new commandant or my loyalty? Or what? I miss you terribly. It's not fair. I've done a few good things with my unit that have taken the pressure off our supplies. The news from the north isn't good. I won't have Ulster carved up like some fat blood pudding. Some for them, some for us. No. If this goes on much longer, I'm just going to buy a train ticket north and be with you forever. Nothing much makes any sense.

Please don't leave me. I'm trying everything I can. I love you more now than I did that day at the National Library, more than at the train station. Your locket is always with me. You are always in my heart.

Your loving Husband,
Danny

21 October 1921,
Cullyhanna, Co. Armagh

Danny boy,

Well, old son, it's been too long, I guess. I know I haven't been good with the letter writing, but there you are. Never was my strong suit, as you know. The wife is helping me with this one, so it might make some sort of sense. There's a lot to say. We'll have it posted from Dundalk. Friendlier there, with the people we both know.

The news from up here is bad, sorry to say. We haven't been able to show our faces in Cross for some time, although Jack's wife and small ones have been left alone—so far. I've been marked by the Specials and the Tommies, to boot, so we've been living in a place you know in the glens. I think that maybe our Inniskeen friends have something to do with it. That's a problem we'll have to take care of when the time comes.

I'm really confused about all the wind and ink coming out of Dublin and London. What, exactly, are they negotiating over there? How come Dev isn't there? What's Collins doing with Griffith and his lot? I'd like to know what they're doing for Ulster. Before he left for England, I hadn't heard or seen a wisp of the Big Fella. All I got was directives from the little fella, Mulcahy. The hold fast orders don't make any sense to us.

In fact, I had to go against them two weeks ago. Father Murtagh was at a hurley match in Strabane— he knows best why—and the Specials scooped him. Word is he made some sort of speech that they thought was anti-British. Good on him, but it's lucky they didn't shoot him on the spot. Anyway, I took some of the lads up there and got him out. We did for a few of the Bs as well, but then they shot three civilians as payback. Anyway, Father Murtagh is back in Dundalk, all safe. I tried to tell him to stay out of Armagh or Derry for the time being, but it's like talking to a brick wall with a collar on. Hard to know what Mulcahy will have to say.

Then we knocked over one of their outposts near Cullaville. Set it alight after we got the arms. Good thing they don't know the glens like we do. They grabbed five of our lads and reinforcements moved in, so we couldn't help them. Sorry to say, from a hedgerow I watched them being shot, one by one. I'll not forget that soon.

The B-Specials, the Tommies and the Loyalist Volunteer Force are laws unto themselves here. I've heard they're forming some kind of new police force as well. We both know who will be in that—and who won't.

I'm biding my time about the doings in Dublin and London, but I don't think I know enough at all. I'd like to hear your views. Not one of us here will go for a divided country, no matter what Lloyd George and his dogs say. That's not what we fought for. What you fought for.

Seems to me that it might be time for you to make a trip back north. One young lady would probably like that.

Soon or Never, Danny, Soon or Never.

Your brother,
Mick

October passed into November. Peace negotiations continued in London; the Irish delegates ferrying back and forth to Dublin. Talk was of a treaty, but no one really knew for a certainty what was being discussed. Even the newspapers seemed confused, or reluctant, or misinformed. For Danny Kavanagh, it was a time of no time, like glue from the hoof of a horse. Hours seemed days, days strung into agonizing weeks, months, of inactivity. He had reached the end of his patience, the end of his ability to cope with a situation he knew was out of his hands. His anger, for the first time in years, had no clear target. His frustration knew no pale. The old dream returned in vivid detail. It had gotten more elaborate over the years: his mother keening over the letter, his brother at Boland's Mill, Devlin by the Fane, the two policemen in the cemetery, the crows, the detective in the brown suit and Charlie's face as he shot him, then O'Neill, Smythe, Charlie Dolan, himself, the funeral, Mrs. Dolan's voice, Bloody Sunday; a litany of pain, pistol shots and accusation. He tried, and failed, to banish them with her face.

The men of Cork No. 2 Brigade refused to let the rumors of what a treaty would bring dampen their spirits, although there was a fatalistic undercurrent of fear that it would come to nothing—as it always had. Off duty, the Irish flowed, the black stout was never far off, and the music, always the music of defiance, defeat, sorrow, victory over the next rise. At first, his men, mostly local, were resentful of an outsider giving them orders, but his leadership in ammunition raids, seeming imperviousness to bullets, lack of fear, and, most of all, his legendary status as a survivor of the GPO, made them obey him as if he was the spreading dark pool of history. They believed, with the certainty of all soldiers in all wars, the scuttlebutt about their mysterious scarred lieutenant from so far in the north. Within weeks, his nickname was the "Avenging Apostle." Awe about Bloody Sunday and the secret war surrounded him like a halo. That did not prevent two of his sergeants, Ross McHugh and Pedar Connor, and Lieutenant Joe McKenna, from mocking his sharp Armagh accent with soft, broad southern vowels.

The three were the brigade musicians—at least they were the best among many—and could set up a considerable racket on a Saturday night in barracks with nothing much else to do. Lately, their restlessness and apprehension had surfaced in the choice of songs; their memories were long.

The ballads gave way to jigs and reels played with passionate intensity.

"Come now, Danny, give us a song then. Somethin about the Gap of Armagh and the smugglers, or the fair sheep of Crossmaglen. Somethin to warm the cockles of the Cork man's stony heart. Somewhere in the key of A flat, if you please." Joe McKenna, cousin to Liam Lynch, was a thorough product of the revivalist Gaelic League. Black haired, stocky, with eyes dark as a well, he could play the Uilleann pipes like a banshee. A Fenian of the old, uncompromising, pitiless sort, he and Danny understood each other from the moment they met. His Gaelic was passing good. Pedar Connor, a Kilkenny man, played the penny whistle with such subtlety and grace that it brought tears to the eyes, while Ross McHugh handled the bodhrán, the Irish drum, with the driving dexterity of a devil. Fiddles, mandolins, a squeezebox, guitars seemed to appear out of nowhere among the listeners. All thirty of them in the room that night watched the Avenging Apostle for his reaction. He couldn't play an instrument, they knew, but they also knew he had a fine voice. Only the coaxing was necessary—and a glass or two of the Irish.

"Not tonight, Joe. I'll not be goin on with 'The Men of County Cork' again to swell yer heads even more. Just not in the mood. Get one of the other lads, there's a good man."

From across the room, Liam Lynch pulled the pipe from his mouth. "Come, Danny, give us a song like a good lad. Pick your own. One that fits your mood. This lot can't sing a note, especially my cousin there. Show em what Armagh's made of."

Danny stared into his half full glass with a frown that made his scar seem even deeper. He held it in his left hand, because the index and middle fingers of his right were scrubbing his thumb—hard—as if he was trying to wipe his fingerprint away. The habit started just after he arrived in Cork, only occasional at first, then more and more often. It had become his trademark among his men.

Finally, he looked to Lynch and said, wearily, "Well, if you'd like, sir." Then, his face brightened in a wicked flash of the old, mischievous Danny Kavanagh. "I'll just test their memories a bit." He bent and spoke to McKenna, who raised his eyebrows then turned to whisper to McHugh and Connor. Connor smiled and fingered his instrument; McHugh scratched his head and shrugged. McKenna started, fingers flying, the pipes screaming with the rage of ages. He nodded to Danny, and the Avenging Apostle began in a deep, quick tenor, the drum and the whistle joining in the with pipes as he sang. The pace, the rhythm, the march, the reel, increased and increased. It was an old song of ancient war. He almost spit the words:

> *Lift, Mac Cahir Oge your face*
> *Brooding o'er the old disgrace*
> *That Black Fitzwilliam stormed your place*
> *And drove you to the fern.*
> *Grey said victory was sure,*
> *Soon the firebrand he'd secure,*
> *Until he met at Glenmalure*
> *With Feagh Mac Hugh O'Byrne.*
>
> *Curse and swear, Lord Kildare,*
> *Feagh will do what Feagh will dare.*
> *Now, Fitzwilliam, have a care,*
> *Fallen is your star low.*
> *Up with halberd, out with sword,*
> *On we go for by the Lord,*

Feagh Mac Hugh has given the word,
"Follow me up to Carlow."

See the swords of Glen Imaal
Flashing o'er the English Pale
See all the children of the Gael
Beneath O'Byrne's banners.
Rooster of a fighting stock
Would you let a Saxon cock
Crow out upon an Irish rock?
Fly up and teach him manners.

When the second chorus began, every man in the room was on his feet singing, rising to a shout in "Follow me up to Carlow." Then silence fell for Danny's last verse:

From Trassagart to Clonmore
There flows a stream of Saxon gore.
Great is Rory Oge More
At sending the loons to Hades.
White is sick and Grey is fled,
Now for Black Fitzwilliam's head.

We'll send it over, dripping red,
To Liza and her ladies.

The musicians took over before the final chorus, raising the tempo impossibly higher, fiddles joining in from around the room. It was a crescendo of pride, defiant, indomitable, angry, victorious. In Elizabethan times, the reel drove the troops to frenzy. In Lloyd George's time, it did exactly the same. Danny changed the words to the last chorus. The crowd did not join in until the final, thunderous, deafening line:

Curse and swear, over there,
We will do what we will dare.
Now, old kingdom, have a care,
Fallen is your star low.
Up with rifle, out with sword,
On we go for by the Lord,
Liam Lynch will give the word,
"Follow me up to Carlow."

Faces flushed, eyes shining, lips taut, the brigade roared in joy, frustration, uncertainty, when the last of note of the pipes died away.

Ross McHugh placed his drum on the floor next to his chair, took a sip of Beamish, considering just a moment. In turn, he bent his head to Pedar Connor, then stood to sing by himself. McHugh's pace was slow; his voice a rich baritone. The whistle, his only accompaniment, was tuned in the key of D:

'Twas down by the glenside,
I met an old woman,
A plucking young nettles,
Nor thought I was coming;
I listened a while
to the song she was humming,
"Glory O, glory O,
To the bold Fenian men.

"When I was a colleen
Their marching and drilling
Awoke by the glenside
Sounds awesome and thrilling,

But they loved dear old Ireland
And to die they were willing,
Glory O, glory O,
To the bold Fenian men.

"Some died by the glenside,
Some died amid strangers,
And wise men have told us
Their cause was a failure;
But they stood by dear Ireland
And never feared danger,
Glory O, glory O,
To the bold Fenian men."

I passed on my way,
God be praised that I met her,
Be life long or short,
I shall never forget her;
We may have great men,
But we'll never have better.
"Glory O, glory O,
To the bold Fenian men."

The room was empty. Danny Kavanagh and the rest of the men of Cork No. 2 Brigade of the Irish Republican Army had gone to their beds. Liam Lynch, their Commander and a member of the Supreme Council of the Irish Republican Brotherhood, took the cold, sour pipe from his mouth and stared out the window into the rain chill of a dark November night. His voice was like a sigh: "Don't let us down, Mick Collins. Don't cave in. There'll be hell to pay."

"Sir, er, Liam, I mean. You wanted to see me?"

"Right. I think it's time you knew that your orders to come down here weren't issued by Collins. It was Mulcahy, and he specifically said you weren't to have leave. He didn't trust you about the Devlin business up north. Said you might run amok. I've seen enough of you to know that won't happen, and you really should have told me how many years it's been. So, the hell with it. This gives you six weeks leave. You, of any man here, deserve it, but you'll have to cut it short if things blow up in London. Be damned careful the closer you get to Ulster. I've a letter here for your brother. Ask him to carefully consider what it says. You're welcome to read it as well, but not now. Then I want you both and Matt O'Faolain to meet with Seamus Woods, OC, Third Northern Division, about what it says. For me, and I know for you, Ireland, a free Ireland, has thirty-two counties, not even one less.

"Oh, yes, and Kavanagh, I don't have to tell you to stay well clear of Inniskeen and Crossmaglen. Dundalk is as far as your orders authorize you; get Mick to meet you there. Woods will get there, too. One more thing, keep a low profile. We don't want your good friends the Devlins to know you're about. Agreed?"

Danny could not help the broad smile, the sunny breaking of a face set hard by the years, the blood, the images. "Would a wire be alright, Liam? I'll have to let her know. And a certain Jim Murtagh."

"Fine, but no last name, nothing into Armagh. Don't send anything until you're well clear of here. We're not sure who's listening up there. You'll remember about the Devlins?"

"So far as I'm able, sir, but what if they come after me?"

"Then you'll do what you must, no doubt. Just don't go after them. You'll have to deal with them eventually, but not just yet. On your way, man." Liam Lynch smacked him on the shoulder, then offered his long, bony hand. "Perhaps I should be the first to offer my congratulations, Danny. Come, man, shake, and learn to leave your damned thumb alone."

On the day he left Mitchelstown, Danny put on the civilian clothes Charlie Dolan had given him. He hadn't been out of uniform since time out of mind. The Webley was back under his left arm, the Walther strapped to his calf. He shaved, looking in the mirror at his set, lowering face, mouth in a habitual frown. "Her last letter didn't say anything, really, but I could tell how angry she was. Maybe she's thought better of it. Or maybe Mary was right; I'm not good enough for her. Or maybe I just don't know. Or maybe I'm crazy." The questions and doubts stayed with him, became more plausible, on the way to Dublin and the north. He was scared.

Joe McKenna drove him to the railway station in Cork City. Danny's men had collected ten pounds as a wedding present. He left off scrubbing his thumb just long enough for a hearty handshake with McKenna as he boarded the train. It was November 16th, 1921. Danny Kavanagh was twenty-five.

8. "CENTRE TO THE SEA"

Danny stopped in Dublin only long enough to make his train connection north. Lynch hadn't ordered him to, so he didn't report to Mulcahy. No survivors of the Twelve Apostles seemed to be in town. He felt like a ghost, especially when he visited the graves in Glasnevin. Hunger striker Tom Ashe was first; the tortured Dick McKee second; Apostle Charlie Dolan the last. On his own for the first time in many long months, he was less and less sure what to do. The dream had become a constant accusation. It would not let him rest. He wrote one letter, to Jim Murtagh, asking to meet with him—alone—before seeing her. The letter was brief, clipped, impersonal. He gave no reason—for the meeting or the location.

Father Murtagh crossed the River Boyne with a private prayer for the fallen and parked the car on Peter Street in the drab, steep, river-bank town of Drogheda. He glanced across at Millmount Fort, high on the hill, and thought the steel step of Oliver Cromwell's righteous iconoclasts still echoed. He looked to St. Laurence Gate, the black stone barbican that Danny and Mick used as a landmark when they were running north from Dublin in 1916, and considered the state of his religion in the 13th century. He hadn't seen Danny, spoken face to face, since Dublin in 1918. Lately, his letters had become increasingly disjointed, verging on panic. Jim Murtagh wondered what he would find; the bold Fenian man or a broken child. Turning away, he walked toward the Westcourt Hotel, holding an angry conversation with himself.

"Now what," he thought, "is all this about? He can't be having cold feet at this late date. Impossible. What else, then? Damn the man. Can't he just get on with it?" His inner tone softened, "Have a care, *Father* Murtagh, he's young yet, and he's been through too much for any man, of any age."

Murtagh stood in the doorway of the hotel restaurant watching Danny. He was sitting alone at a table in the crowded room, staring into space, frowning brow knit, brooding. Again and again, the index and middle fingers of his right hand slid over his thumb with such force that the veins on the back of his hand stood out proud. His head snapped around quickly, eyes squinting sharply, when the waitress brought his meal. She flinched at the scar. Jim

Murtagh considered the fair, damaged face, as the brooding returned and the fingers angrily scrubbed his thumb. The scar, he thought, would always be heartbreaking, like the smack of the banshee, but it was no longer so puckered, purple, so horrible. It had become part of him. The priest recognized with a start that Danny had chosen a good defensive position. He sat in a corner, his back to the wall, and he had a clear view of all the doors and windows. He knew Danny would be armed. Jim Murtagh began to understand.

"I was fortunate, Danny. Once he finished tearing a strip off me over my Strabane exploits, Archbishop Sullivan gave us a choice of places. We can stay at a house near Monasterboice—it's an old cemetery with some very fine crosses and a round tower—or we can go to Newgrange, in the town. Newgrange is a bit close to Slane Hill and bloody King Billy, so maybe you might prefer Monasterboice. Your choice."

Danny quickly turned his head to look out the window of the car. His voice was hoarse. "No, not the cemetery. I'll explain later. Newgrange'll do. And thanks, Jim."

"Newgrange it'll be. There's no need to thank me, but I'm bound to say all this mystery has me a bit worried." That was all he thought he should say. The trip was completely silent thereafter. The priest watched as Danny's fingers resumed on his thumb, the skin squeaking, rippling with the force.

"That's the lot, Jim. Devlin you know about, of course. Then, fourteen altogether in Dublin. Operations in Cork and Boland's Mill? Hard to say for certain, but I don't count them the same. That's war on the barricades, in the fields, the barracks. I'm just not sure what to call the Dublin ones. Some people, the papers, the English, Unionists, call them murder. My brother did for the two peelers in the cemetery, so I didn't want to go back there. It's a very strange place. I can hear those damned crows in my sleep. Mick said the Faery was about, and I believe it."

"Danny, I don't think my judgment—officially, at least—has changed since we first talked. From a moral and ethical point of view, I mean. Unofficially is another matter. Think, man, about where we'd be if you and your squad hadn't done what you did—under legitimate orders from the freely elected government of your country. That's the key. We'd still be under Dublin Castle's boot; in the same prostrate position we've been in for centuries. Look at what you've done, accomplished. You and people like Collins, McKee, Mulcahy, Lynch, Dalton, even your Joe McKenna down in Cork, have fought the mighty Empire to a standstill. We just might turn out to be a nation some day—depending—God willing. Of course, I can't share what you've seen and heard. The faces must haunt you."

"Haunt? That's not the half of it. It's like they're all inside me, living one minute, crying, dying the next, taking parts of me with them to the grave. Some nights, I'm afraid to close my eyes. Sure, I can argue with myself about legitimate orders and all, but that doesn't stop the faces, the sounds, the blood, the dream. The smell of a dying man's blood can't be forgotten.

"And now? Everybody seems ready to go for each other's throats. Some are for the truce; some aren't. How come de Valera signed it on Lloyd George's terms? Liam Lynch doesn't seem to trust anybody outside Cork. What the hell is Collins doing with Arthur Griffith in London? If they give away Ulster, I'll....I don't know what I'd do. Who's in charge? Who's giving the damned orders, anyway? Lynch? Mulcahy? Dev? The Big Fella? Cathal Brugha? I'm not sure anymore. If there's no one in charge, then what I did really was murder. I can't live with that—or expect her to, either."

Jim Murtagh went to the mahogany sideboard and poured two stiff measures of Irish whiskey into cut crystal. He paused a moment, studying the Webley and the Walther lying on the polished top in their smooth leather holsters. The butts were worn. Tools of the trade, well used, well oiled. He knew the man was tearing himself apart, but reaching out with compassion probably wouldn't work with a tribal warrior like Danny Kavanagh. Deliberately, he decided to let his own frustration loose for a change. Murtagh sat heavily, exhaled through his nose, held out a glass to the tormented soul sitting opposite him and began. As he listened, Danny unconsciously switched the glass from his right hand to his left, so his fingers could wipe out his thumbprint.

"Right. I'll play the Jesuit again. Just sit still and quiet for a moment. All that is hindsight, and you know it. Self pity is not one of your most admirable attributes. Within the limits of what you knew—and believed—in Dublin, you acted in a just cause, your country's cause. We've always skirted the issue, but we shouldn't. You committed no sin. Those British agents in the Cairo Gang would have killed you if they could in what they probably believed was the service of their country. Think of what they did to Dick McKee. You killed them in what you believed—and believe still, I think—is the service of your country. And let's not forget the long delayed justice for centuries of slaughter from them. I'll not speak for the Castle's Irish spies in the Igoe Gang. Their motive seems to be only greed.

"Then is not now—today. But that's not the real issue at present, and, if you'll forgive me, it just burns my arse. You do not have the right to go back on your word to her. That, my man, *that*, would be a sin in any religion you care to name. She considers you her husband as much as if you took the vows before God. And so, Danny Kavanagh, do you. You can't let some misguided sense of gallantry or fear or shame ruin your life—and hers. I can't permit that. Perhaps the uncertainty, the guilt, will never go away. Maybe the risk will always be there. Learn to live with it. You went in with your eyes open, remember? If you don't come north with me and stand up at the altar like a man, you'll never be one again, so help me God.

"No, don't say anything. I'm not finished. On the political side, try to think about someone other than yourself for a change. Sorry, that was uncalled for. What I mean is, try to think in broader terms than army terms. First of all, what's going on is very dangerous for all of us. Believe me, I'm not the only one in Ireland who thinks that. You've said it's well known that de Valera has no power over the IRA and hardly the IRB. Have you considered what that might mean? If there's no government in charge—freely elected—then the will of the people has nothing to do with anything. What we'll have is a military dictatorship; same thing we've had all along, just different uniforms. That can't be allowed.

"Second. If there's a treaty, and it looks like there will be, part or all of Ulster will remain in English hands. As I've said before, that's flat. Any Boundary Commission won't change it. Craig and Carson in Belfast have Lloyd George exactly where they want him. There'll be no compromise. None. The British electorate would dump him in a second if he did, the Ulster Unionist MPs would withdraw their support and the government would fall. Once done, it will be next to impossible to undo. Don't forget, the English public are still smarting about the glorious deeds of the Tans and Auxies.

"Third. We have to think very carefully about what any treaty will mean, will say. The English won't just let the southern counties walk out of Empire to become an independent country. That won't happen now; maybe never will. Think about your history, man. They won't have a hostile country, small or no, on their flank. You'll recall it was German arms the *Aud* was supposed to bring for the Rising, and Casement landed from a German submarine. That means the oath to the King stays and we remain part of Empire, just with a different status, like Canada, perhaps. That's my interpretation of the immediate future, no matter what Collins, Griffith or even de Valera say publicly.

"The real question, the only question, really, is what the IRA will do about it, and, more importantly, how the IRB will respond. Some will be for the treaty as the best of a bad lot and settle for getting the English out of the south; some will never give up the old dream. Unfortunately, you are one of the dreamers. God help me, so am I. I don't relish the consequences. There, I'm done. Feels better, too, getting all that off my chest. First time."

Danny sat staring into his glass, nodding his head, fingers busy, thinking, trying to rein in the chaos of his thoughts, make sense of the tumble of images, words, responsibilities, loyalties, memories, desires. Jim Murtagh filled Danny's glass again. Danny did not want to look him in the eye, so he said into the amber reflection in his left hand.

"You know, Jim, outside my brothers, my father and mother, rest them, Sophie, I don't think I've ever had a true friend. Comrades, yes, true friends, no." He looked up, green eyes steady, clear, and raised his glass. "*Sláinte*," he said, in Gaelic.

"*Sláinte va*," Murtagh replied, knowing the toast said he was ready to go—to her. "You know, Danny boy, I think we deserve more than a few of these this night. We've—or at least I've—about covered the military and political sides of the question. Tomorrow, though, we have to make plans and have a talk about a few things on the religious side of the equation. Took the liberty of reading the first banns when I got your wire from Cork City. When was the last time you went to confession? Have to ask. My job."

"Aye, thought so, Jim. Guess it'll have to be. Can't recall."

"Yes, it'll have to be. That part's out of my hands, Danny. We'll be going to Carlingford, by the way, not Dundalk. Too public."

"Grand, it's a sweet little town, that, right on the lough. I'll invite *Cúchulainn* and Queen Maeve down from that turf bog high on the mountain for a jar."

"Good plan, Danny, good plan. Never hurts to have the old Irish on hand for a blessing. We'll leave the Kavanagh banshee off the list, though, if you're willing."

"Believe me, Jim, the banshee's knock is the last thing I want to hear."

Jim Murtagh reached over and clasped the top of Danny's right hand to stop the fingers.

It was dark. The tide was in. The wind slashed off Carlingford Lough with a saber's whistle. Danny stood by the stone sea wall, watching the white caps rising, only to have their heads cut off by the gale, and the tiny, helpless fishing smacks trying duck the blade and survive the swell. Across the water, close, he could see the black humps of the Mourne

Mountains, at their feet the lights of Rostrevor and Warrenpoint. He stood in County Louth, one of the fortunate counties, Slieve Foy at his back. Warrenpoint and Rostrevor were in County Down, Ulster. His fingers were busy again.

She was on him before he knew it, punching his back, crying. Theirs was less a meeting of long separated lovers than a collision of Irish tides at the "swallow of the sea" between Country Antrim, far in the north, and the Mull of Kintyre in Scotland.

"Damn you, Danny Kavanagh, damn you. I thought you'd never come back to me. I pictured you dead, with a bullet in your heart. Damn you for a pagan." She started to laugh, hysterically, relieved. "But now you're safe, here, with me, for good and all." Her head was buried in his chest. With the point of its sword, the wind lifted her shawl and threw it aside. Strands of her loosened black hair flew in the hiss of spray.

"Shush, now, my love. It's alright at last. All home, all safe. Let's get the hell out of the weather. I've a thirst coming on."

"Not likely, *Mister* Kavanagh. Not just yet."

They kissed to swallow time apart; the urgency of the unconsummated; the awkwardness of virginity. He could feel her, every warm curve from chest to thigh, pressed hard, tense against him as if she were trying to take a pattern of his body. The wet smell of sweet soap in her hair. She could feel the muscles of his arms, his chest, his groin, the strength of his hands, taking a pattern of hers. Both were ready, impatient, driven to mate, blood to blood.

"Well, now, so this is the young hero who fought for his religion at the Dublin Post Office, is it? You'll be feeling doubly proud today, Kavanagh, your bride is as beautiful as she is devout. I'm still not so sure about the speed with which the banns were read, but we live in modern times, so we do."

Archbishop Sullivan held out his hand for Danny to kiss the ring. Danny looked quickly to Father Murtagh sitting at the head table, shrugged, and gave Sullivan a hearty handshake, then dropped the hand like a stone. "Right, padre, whatever you say. Back in a tick."

As he made for the table, and his wife, he could see the grimace on Jim Murtagh's face. He smiled broadly, whacked his friend on the back and said, "There, how'd I do? Saved, you think?"

"Damnation, Danny, have a care. He's an Archbishop, after all."

"Well, now, and so? I shook the man's hand like a gentleman, didn't I? Fightin fer the faith and all. So that's what I did? News to me. Alright, Jim, no more. I'll act the best Catholic this day."

Murtagh growled, but he smiled quickly. "By the Lord, Danny, you are one unredeemable renegade, that's certain."

The best man, Mick Kavanagh, wobbled to the table. "Hey, there, ye old married fart, ye. Are ye gettin?"

"I'm gettin, yer man, when ye step to the bar and fetch me a jar." Danny stood behind his wife, put his hands on her shoulders and kissed the top of her head through the lace. Her hands leaped to his. She wore her mother's and grandmother's wedding dress, white satin aged to rich ivory, with tiny seed pearls around the high, lacy neck. It was sewn in 1856; the quiet grace of the 19th century. He whispered in her ear, "Are ye happy, then, missus?"

She turned to him, blushing: "God knows you are a stupid man. Not quite yet, entirely. Go way with the lads, *Mister* Kavanagh. Give a married woman some peace."

He walked toward his brother and Matt O'Faolain, who were leaning against the restaurant bar of the Carlingford Arms. On his way through the small crowd, he stopped to salute the maid of honor, Mary O'Faolain of the flaming red mane and indomitable mouth. She stood chatting pleasantly to the Archbishop. With them was her oldest brother, Father Liam, a Redemptorist monk who came down from the Clonard in Belfast for the occasion. "Excuse me, there, padre," Danny said to Sullivan, "This'll just take a sec." He put one arm around her waist, pulled her to him and quickly kissed her squarely on the mouth. "How do, sister in law. I'm not such a bad sort, after all, now am I?"

"Danny, don't you dare, you, you...." Mary started to laugh, but put her hand to her mouth when she saw the horrified look on Sullivan's face. Father Liam looked on with a bright grin and tipped his glass in Danny's direction. Danny turned to Sophia; she had her hands pressed together in prayer, looking up at the low, brown ceiling timbers, but her body was shaking with laughter.

Big Matt O'Faolain's face was almost as red as the flaming bush of his eyebrows. Mick Kavanagh was not far behind him in liquor. Danny, for his part, was too ecstatic, still wondering at his immense good fortune, too much the center of attention, too at peace, too excited, anticipating, to spend much time over his jar. Matt O'Faolain took Danny's hand in his beefy farmer's grip. With the other, he slapped him hard on the back. "There's a good man, yerself. And yer welcome to the family, boyo. Just lay off the Irish today, there's a good lad. You've got yer work cut out for ye, this night." Mick laughed roughly, so did Danny, but he dropped his head, embarrassed.

O'Faolain cleared his throat. "Just a bit a fun, Danny. No harm. She'll make a good wife, so she will, even with the strong head she's got on her shoulders. I've done me best to bring her up right, with the right ideas in her sweet head, since her ma died. Not done too badly, if I do say so meself. She might even reform a pagan from Crossmaglen, I've heard. Stranger things have happened, they say. Not to spoil the festivities at all, but we three should just step into the public bar for a tick. I'd like a quick word."

Danny turned to Sophia as the three men stepped through the doorway. She was looking intensely at him; so was Jim Murtagh. His face showed concern, turning to understanding.

Hers was creased in fear. She looked to her priest when she lost sight of them amid the noisy crowd in the next room.

"Sophie, there's nothing to be done about that. They're soldiers, after all."

"I know, Father, but I don't want to lose him now, after all this time. I don't want to lose any of them—no more—none. It's not right that Jack's wife refused to come, is it?"

"Perhaps, Sophie, but I spoke to her when I was on my way down from Strabane. I think she just can't bear the memories. She blames Danny, and to a lesser extent, Mick, for Jack's death. I don't have to tell you that's not the case, but there's nothing to be done right now. Armagh people are difficult to figure out, no mistake. Nothing to do with you, at all. I'm certain she meant no insult."

"I'm so pleased, Father, that Danny made his confession to you and took the sacrament today. There's hope for him yet," she said with a small, sly smile.

"Don't go countin yer chickens, girl, there's a good lass. Danny did what he had to do—for you, even for me. You might want to make a permanent vocation of it, your choice, but I think yon Danny Kavanagh is unreformable, a fine man, a firm friend, but unreformable in that way, at least. Even so, he'll make a good, strong husband, father good, strong sons and daughters. It's up to you to raise them right. Lord, what is it now?"

Sophia Kavanagh was blushing like a hot summer sunset hissing into the ocean. It was more noticeable, perhaps, because of the whiteness of her skin, the deep blue of her eyes, and the shining rope of black hair with its white banshee flash. She looked at the open palms of her hands crossed in her lap.

"I'll have none of that, my girl. It's only natural, as you well know. Don't doubt yourself; you'll be fine, just fine. Listen, the lads have started with the old woman's song. I hope old Ireland has her wits about her and asks the right questions in the days ahead."

The small public bar was crammed with Armagh men from Mick's brigade and County Louth men under Matt O'Faolain's command. The talk was loud, the music even louder. Danny hadn't seen the Crossmaglen contingent since early 1916; the Louth lads since the RIC raid in Blackwater. It was like a homecoming. There was a shout of approval when they entered the room, glasses raised, *sláinte* from every corner. The song started near the piano, just a few voices at first, then the room took it up with a roar, the Armagh IRA taking one line, the Louth IRA the next. Boots stomping in time on the stone floor, they tried to out shout each other in memory of the doomed 1798 Rising:

"The French are on the sea," says the Shan van Voght,
"The French are on the sea," says the Shan van Voght,
"The French are in the bay, they'll be here at break of day,
And the Orange will decay," says the Shan van Voght,
"And the Orange will decay," says the Shan van Voght.

"And where will they have their camp?" says the Shan van Voght,
"And where will they have their camp?" says the Shan van Voght.
"On the Curragh of Kildare, and the boys will all be there

With their pikes in good repair," says the Shan van
Voght,

"With their pikes in good repair," says the Shan van
Voght.

"And what will the yeomen do?" says the Shan van
Voght,

"And what will the yeomen do?" says the Shan van
Voght,

"What will the yeomen do but throw off the red and
blue

And swear they will be true to the Shan van Voght,

And swear they will be true to the Shan van Voght."

"Then what colour will be seen?" says the Shan van
Voght,

"Then what colour will be seen?" says the Shan van
Voght,

"What colour should be seen where our fathers'
homes have been

But our own immortal green?" says the Shan van

Voght.
"But our own immortal green?" says the Shan van
Voght.

"Will old Ireland then be free?" says the Shan van
Voght,
"Will old Ireland then be free?" says the Shan van
Voght
"Old Ireland shall be free from the centre to the sea;
Then hurrah for liberty," says the Shan van Voght.

"First things first, boys. Two days ago, I took a few of our men and went over to Inniskeen and had a talk with the Devlins. There was a lot of bluster, big chests, hands under the coat and all, but I set them straight. The old man, Eddie and Pete's father, Mike's the name, seems to be the one with the most hate on, though the three other sons are about the same, uncles, cousins, hangabouts, too.

"I told them flat, that if they ever came near you boys or my girl, I would personally see to it that the Devlin name died out, quick. Not only that, privately I mentioned to the old man that if they kept on as informers for the B-Specials, I wouldn't be at all surprised if their smuggling business didn't dry up like cow shite. After all, I said, I didn't have any control over the Armagh Brigade. They aren't very bright, the lot of them, but I think I got the message through their beech heads.

"Next off. We've all read Liam Lynch's letter to Mick. In a few days, once the blushing bridegroom can tear his mind away from other things, we should sit down and talk about what we're going to do—or not do—as the case may be. Then we should meet with Woods, like Lynch said. Agreed?"

Faces set, the three IRA officers shook hands in turn. Their soldiers watched.

"Fine, then. Off you go, Danny, back to the bride. For today, at least, I'm the father in law, and what I say goes." Danny stepped back into the restaurant, a barrage of applause, whistles and good natured leers launched at his back.

She sat at the dressing table in the finest hotel room in Carlingford, wearing a long-sleeved, white cotton nightgown buttoned to the neck. The fabric was very fine, almost sheer. Her feet were bare on the thick oriental carpet. A comfortable

coal fire burned bright in the iron grate, casting broad
shadows from the bars. No other light, except from the
brilliant moon. Their large room was on the third floor. She
had pulled back the curtains from the high, multi-paned
windows that looked out on the black ruin of King John's Fort
and the lough. The sea was calm for winter; an enormous
white disk trembled in the heaving mercury.

Her hair was down. She brushed it with long strokes,
dreaming, worrying into the beveled oval mirror attached to
the black-varnished dressing table. In front of her, spread like
a fan, her most precious possessions, the ivory comb, the cut
crystal jar with the silver rim she used to store the hair from
the ivory brush she was using, the mother of pearl rosary
blessed at Fatima, her missal with its white leather covers, gilt
edges and red ribbon bookmark, the tortoiseshell hair clips,
the pincushion, hat pins with jet heads in a matching glass
dish. She could feel him behind her. He came to her, put his
hands on her shoulders, then took the brush and kissed the
top of her head. Their eyes met in the glass, blue on green,
dancing, alive, frightened, expectant.

She looked down at her hands, turning the shining gold
band on the finger of her left, watching the sparkle of the red

stone in the engagement ring on her right. He had given it to her two days before they married. Jim Kavanagh had bought it for him in Dundalk. "Danny, tell me true. Did you ever...? Have you ever...? I mean, like when you were in Dublin all that time? I've heard about the women there. Mary told me."

His hands tightened on her shoulders, feeling the heat through the cotton, then moving to massage her neck. The old mischievous look returned. "Ah, well, as to that. Of course. Hundreds of times. Towards the last, down in Cork, every night. You know what we men are like."

He could feel her go rigid under his touch. Her look was hurt, pouting bottom lip trembling, a child still. "Danny, no, say it isn't so. Please. For me."

He smiled into her eyes, then turned away and sat on the high bed with its spool-turned mahogany headboard. She could see his reflection. "Yes, my love, hundreds of times—in my mind. Every time it was you, only you." Her look implored him.

"What a question to ask a man on his wedding night." His head sank to his chest, then he looked up at her, a mild, soft look on his face. "The answer is no. I haven't." The spark came back. "And you, woman? What about you."

"Danny Kavanagh, don't you dare. What do you think I am? Really, now."

He laughed out loud. "Ah, I see. Turnabout isn't fair play, then? I'll have to reconsider this marriage business." His smile was broad, mocking.

She looked at him with her head tilted to one side, then laughed in turn. She stood from the table, her back to him. He could not see her reflection. She looked down and started undoing the buttons. The nightgown fell away. The black hair smoothing down her back, the sinuous line from ribs to waist to hips, were the most extraordinarily beautiful images he had ever seen. Her skin in the firelight was white and smooth as fine, new satin. She could hear the intake of breath.

Sophia turned to him, head down, face shrouded by her black mane. Her right hand covered one heavy breast, the forearm crossed over the other, the left hand between her legs. She looked at him through her hair, coyly, embarrassed, hoping, searching his face. Then she met his green, green eyes; hers darkened to a shade he did not know—but understood at once. Her arms moved to her sides as she walked to him. Her hands ran through his auburn hair, over his face, his scar, as he sat below her. She pulled him to her; he took her breasts in his hands and kissed them slowly. Her head was thrown back, mouth open, hair cascading behind her as she swayed under his mouth. Then she pushed him gently away. They both knew there was no reason to hurry. They had waited so long.

"Stand up, *Mister* Kavanagh, if you please. The fire's a bit hot, and you've way too much on."

He stood and kissed her mouth, his hands cradling her face. "If there's a God in heaven, *Missus* Kavanagh, he made you the most perfect thing on earth."

"Quiet, if you please, so many buttons and studs," she said as she tossed his shirt on the floor. She looked at his barrel chest, the thick, prominent muscles of his breast. Her hands skimmed slightly over the mat of hair, pushing her locket aside. Her mouth was open slightly, her breath light but rapid. She looked into his face, then took him in her arms, kissing him to the soul. He could feel her legs shaking, parting for him.

He bent and picked her up, curling her to him, kissing her stomach, before laying her on the bed. She did not get under the covers, but watched him take off the rest of his clothes and lay down beside her, wondering at the strength of a man.

He stroked her face gently, then all of her, exploring. Eyes open, she did the same.

"If it's a boy, Danny, we'll call him Jack."

"Yes, my love, it will be a boy, and it will be Jack."

Neither slept that winter night. After the first cries of surprise, pleasure, wonder, there was too much to know, discover, feel, see, experience. The two rushing Irish tides had collided, melded, joined, into the swallow of one turbulent sea.

Daniel Sebastian Kavanagh and Sophia Margaret O'Faolain were married in Carlingford, County Louth, on Tuesday, December 6th, 1921. For their honeymoon, they were to spend two weeks in Tourmakeady, County Mayo, where Sophia was born and her mother buried. Their hotel looked over Lough Mask, at the foot of the Partry Mountains, in one of the most mystical, beautiful places in the world.

On the day they were married, Michael Collins, Arthur Griffith and the delegation from Dublin signed the Anglo-Irish Treaty in London. The English Prime Minister, Lloyd George, played them like the master gambler he was: sign here, now, without going back to Ireland for approval, or risk a total, all-out war of annihilation from the mightiest military power on earth. Ulster was not part of the agreement. The boundary could be settled later, not now.

9. FOUR COURTS

10 February 1922,
Skibbereen, Co. Cork

My love,

Your news is the best I've ever had. Poleaxed, and it feels tremendous. You are a wonder in more ways than just the one. I couldn't figure out why the wind and rain never stopped in Tourmakeady. Now I know. Gave us enough time. It's to be Jack, don't forget, make sure.

Don't pout. I still agree it's a beautiful place, storms and all, especially to make babies in. We'll go back—in fine weather—and make another. Don't blush.

I hope to have leave when you get close to your time. That I wouldn't miss for the world. I'm sure Liam Lynch will agree. I'd like you to think about Joe McKenna as godfather—he's become a true friend— though maybe you'd rather someone from your family. Maybe Father Liam? He's a good sort, that one. Or

Jim Murtagh? No, guess not. He'll be doing the christening, won't he? Say hello for me. I'll be writing him shortly.

Down here, things have gotten worse rather than better. There's a lot of hot talk about overthrowing the Treaty and the Free State. Our brigade wants nothing to do with either one. We want to start over. I just can't believe Michael Collins signed it, even though he said it would give us "the freedom to achieve freedom." That's just not good enough. It's been so long. We're all tired of waiting. You ask about Arthur Griffith. Let's just say I'm not surprised, even though he was sick when he was in London.

Most of the lads down here are more concerned with the terms than the splitting up of Ulster, though Lynch doesn't feel that way. You know where I stand there, same as your father, Mick, Seamus Woods. We talked it over for a long time. I do agree that no matter what happens the Oath to the King has got to go and Ireland is to be a Republic, right out of Empire. Liam Lynch is dead set against the Treaty. We're all with him. He even seems to have come around in favor of President de Valera since he denounced the Treaty and walked out of the debate. That's a surprise. We'll just have to wait and see what happens.

One good thing, at least, about the Treaty is that the Tommies have been pulling out. I wish my father had lived to see them marching out of Skibbereen Barracks, us marching in and raising the Irish flag. It was all very military; uniforms, salutes and swords and such, but not one of my boys could stop grinning. Me, too.

I miss you very much, my wild Mayo girl. Sometimes, waking up next to you is more than I can bear. Alright, I can hear you saying it. I've been trying not to mess about with my fingers any more, but it's a hard habit to break.

Take very, very good care of yourself, or you'll have me to deal with. I'm not much of an authority, but my mother always said porter is good at such times.

Close your eyes and feel me touching you.

Your loving Husband,
Danny

10 March1922,
Skibbereen, Co. Cork

Dear Matt,

Writing as your comrade, not your son in law, to let you know that we've squared off down here. No doubt, you already know that the army has split over the Treaty, just like the government. My brigade has gone completely for the Anti-Treaty side, Republicans to the last man. Even though we might be in the minority in the twenty-six counties, we have to keep faith with 1916 and the rest, like my father. Liam Lynch is working on keeping the army in one piece, but I don't think it will work. Looks like what we decided at the meeting with Woods saw into the future, or maybe it was Liam who knew what would happen. There is no possible way that my Armagh, my Crossmaglen, stay in English hands.

I know we agreed in Dundalk that we'd support Lynch after his letter said he'd never go for a divided country, but maybe I'm a little closer to the situation than you are. Consider this. If Lynch can't reunite the army, there's bound to be a fight. Bound to be. He's on the outs with Tom Barry and Rory O'Connor, too, even though they're against the Treaty. There's so many splits I can't keep it straight.

I can't believe it, us up against the Big Fella and that little fella Mulcahy? Mulcahy I wouldn't mind. Still, it's a hard thought, but it will have to be if we're ever to get rid of the British and put Ulster back together. Be very sure you want in on this. My brother has already said he does. There's not much he'll be able to do on the other side of the border, though. The B-Specials and the UVF will take up a lot of their time.

We've been very busy storing up as much arms as we can find. Word is that Mulcahy's people are getting all sorts of weapons—even heavy guns—from the English. How's that for a history lesson?

We haven't come this far to let them tell us who we are and what we can and can't do. If there's to be more fighting, so be it. I'll take no joy or pride in it, but we haven't won yet, and we must. Give me your thoughts. Forgot to mention I've been promoted.

Éirinn go Brách,
Captain Daniel Kavanagh,
Cork No. 2 Brigade

"Damnation, Danny, I've never seen Liam so angry, and I'm his cousin, for God's sake. We grew up together. You know these Dublin boys better than he does. Are you sure we can do any good? Christ, I've always heard this city's one filthy hole. What a stink from the river. How're we gonna get in? There's a hell of a lot of them. Jaysus, just look at the size of that field gun."

Danny Kavanagh and Joe McKenna stood on Merchants Quay, on the south side of the Liffey, regarding the neoclassical façade and soaring round dome of the Four Courts building on the north bank. Pro-Treaty IRA troops and Dublin Guards were massed at the front. It was early evening, June 24th, 1922, and Anti-Treaty Republicans, led by Dublin No.1 Brigade, had held the Four Courts since mid-April. Liam Lynch wasn't necessarily against a show of resistance to the Treaty, but he considered the move provocative, premature and dangerous. No one wanted civil war. Because of his Dublin connections, he sent Danny Kavanagh to pour water on the burning fuse. McKenna was his back-up. Neither was in uniform.

The heavy guns were sent by the British Army. Lloyd George and Winston Churchill had the Pro-Treaty forces and the Provisional Irish Government in a very awkward position. If they didn't take action against the Anti-Treaty Republican garrison, then Empire troops would be sent in to join the 5,000 that remained in Dublin to remedy the situation—and avenge the bungling IRA assassination of Sir Henry Wilson on the 22nd in London. That would mean a swift end to the Treaty and the men inside the Four Courts. Before he answered McKenna, Danny watched Michael Collins and Richard Mulcahy, both magnificent in full uniform, conferring by themselves across the river in the shelter of a Lancia armored car.

"Well, Joe, can't say for sure. Orders is orders, I guess. Ye give me too much credit. Don't really know anybody in the Dublin No.1 Brigade. Number 2, yes. I was with Paddy Flanagan on Bloody Sunday, don't forget. And I do know those two. Let's go."

"What? Danny, yer crazy. That's the Big Fella himself—and the general. He really is quite the little fella, ain't he? They'll just scoop us up and lock us up, quicker than shite through a goose."

"Maybe, old son, but I don't think so. We go back a long way, and I'm owed." Danny settled the Webley firmly under his arm. His fingers were very busy with his thumb as, in full view, the two emissaries crossed the bridge and approached Collins, the Commander in Chief of the Pro-Treaty, Free-State forces, and Mulcahy, the most powerful general in the country.

Mulcahy saw Danny first. He barked an order and ten soldiers surrounded the two before they got closer than thirty feet—out of effective pistol range for a Webley. "Captain, disarm and detain those men. The one with the scar will have a revolver under his arm and an automatic strapped to his calf. Not sure about the other." He drew large circles in the air with the barrel of his pistol as he said: "What in Christ are you doing here, man?"

Michael Collins turned slowly, wearily, and looked deeply into Danny Kavanagh's eyes across that steel space. The Big Fella's face was putty gray, haggard, an old man at thirty-one. "Hold on, Captain. There's no need for any of that." He turned an imperious look on Mulcahy, then walked toward the two men, brushing his troops aside, extending his hand to Danny. "Well, well, young Kavanagh, it's been a while, hasn't it? Expected a grand entrance on a motorbike, just like old times. How's that girl of yours? O'Faolain, right? A stunner. Who's your mate?"

"Married her, sir, and a wee one on the way. This is Lieutenant Joe McKenna, Cork No. 2. Cousin to Liam Lynch. Look, Mick, it's like this. Liam sent us up here to talk to the people inside, try and find a way out. He's still hoping to reunite the army, and he doesn't like the look of this."

"Married? Fatherhood? Splendid news, young Kavanagh. Good luck to you—and to her. Yours really is a charmed life." He glanced at the graceful Four Courts' façade with a pained expression. "No, I don't like the look of it, either. And you can tell him that. The garrison in there has to end the occupation. That's final, but they don't have to down arms. If they don't stop this, we'll have the English back in here very, very shortly. I'm sure you know what that would mean. Unfortunately, looks like it's gone a bit far for cool heads, no matter what Lynch might—or might not—want. But perhaps it's worth a try. We certainly haven't had any luck thus far.

Captain, give these men safe passage into the building. Take them under a flag of truce. Do it."

General Mulcahy spun on his commander, his pistol lowered to his side: "Mick, what in hell's gotten into you? I've warned you time and time again this Kavanagh is a law unto himself, just like all those lunatics in Armagh." This time the invisible patterns were not identifiable. "They've no patience for anything. He's probably the best shot in the country, and you're going to let him join up with the other side?"

"Dick, without men like Danny Kavanagh and the rest of the Apostles, we'd still be scuttling by the Castle in the dark with our hats pulled over our eyes. He deserves the chance, and he'll have it. Besides, he's not 'the other side,' as you put it. Neither are the men in there; they fought with us, don't forget. If Lynch wants peace, then so do I. Maybe he can even talk sense to Tom Barry and hothead Rory O'Connor. Don't worry, we won't let their lot start shooting up the Tommies that remain in the city. Not today, anyway."

"Christ. Well, disarm them, at least."

"No, Dick, I won't. Kavanagh, same toast as always, 'Long life, a wet mouth, and death in Ireland.' Captain, you heard my orders. Carry them out, if you please."

As they left, Danny turned to Collins and spoke a simple "Why?" into his eyes. It was a large question that encompassed the Treaty, the Free State, the partition of the six counties and looming civil war. The old Mick Collins shrugged, and with a small, boyish smile, said, "Best we could get—for now—Danny. We'll put your Ulster back together soon enough. Have a care, so, father to be."

Danny's mission to extinguish the fuse of civil war failed completely, the more so because not one single officer or group was in command of the Anti-Treaty Republican ranks. All he accomplished was more acrimonious bickering. He wrote to Lynch in despair; no one on the other side seemed to look, though everyone did, when he walked out of the building and boldly dropped it in the letter box still emblazoned with the cast iron British Lion.

The Free State read the ultimatum to the Four Courts at 3:30 in the morning of June 27th. Rejection came quickly, but no one, on either side, wanted to go down in history as the first Irishman to fire on his brothers—this time, at least. It fell to Michael Collins. He knew there was no choice; he had run out of room to maneuver, with Lynch, Barry, O'Connor, Cathal Brugha, with Lloyd George, Winston Churchill. He gave the order, and his troops began shelling the Four Courts with British Army guns at 4:15. Predictably, General Mulcahy insisted the rounds be timed at quarter-hour intervals.

Danny and Joe McKenna sat at their posts by a sandbagged window on the ground floor; their Lee-Enfields propped against the wall. McKenna had tears in his eyes. "Jaysus, Danny, this is crazy. There's our own out there, firing at us, for Christ's sake, not the Tommies, like O'Connor said. We've fucking lost again. This lot in here is so disorganized there's no hope of keeping on for much longer. We'll never be a Republic this way, never. We're right trapped. Shite."

"Yerrah. That we are, Joe, just like the GPO. But we got outta that one and beat the Brits on the streets and in the field. By God, we'll do it again. No matter—no matter at all— what it takes. Word is that Lynch, himself, is in the building. Maybe he can call a halt to all this."

Rory O'Connor, that most Republican of Republicans, walked toward them along the long corridor, arguing with Liam Lynch. When he got close enough, O'Connor roared, "Damn your eyes, Captain Kavanagh, point that weapon and use it. You, too, Lieutenant. What else are ye here for? A rest? We've got enough poor sods that never handled a rifle, damned Trucileers. You two have. Get busy." He turned on Lynch: "So these are your Cork boys, eh? You have my final answer. It's no, not a chance. Those bastards out there are using British guns on us. That's the lot, if you recall, that signed the goddamned Treaty. No. We'll stick here to the last man. If you want out of it, then get the hell out of it. We'll make our Republic our own way—without their help out there—or yours, come to that."

"I'm not interested in a lecture on martyrdom, Rory, or a lesson in stupidity, either. I'm here, aren't I? So are some of my men, like those two there. I'm with you, but we have to get some sort of organization going or we haven't a chance. Cathal Brugha and Dublin No. 1 won't listen to you, and your people won't listen to them. If you want me to help with that, I'm yer man."

"No thank you," O'Connor barked, then stalked off into the dark and smoke. Right on schedule, another shell hit the building. When the deafening, reverberating boom subsided, the sporadic rifle fire returned by the Republicans sounded half-hearted, reluctant. Lynch joined the two men from his brigade at the sandbagged window.

Danny Kavanagh pointed his rifle toward the opposing barricade. It was just coming dawn. In the iron sights of his Lee-Enfield, he saw the pale, drawn face of Paddy Flanagan, his partner on Bloody Sunday, peering around the side of an armored car. Danny lined up to fire. The 303 caliber bullet hit the armor plate six inches above Flanagan's head and sparked off it with a wail. He looked directly at Danny, only some thirty yards away. Danny grinned and waved. Flanagan's head bowed slightly. He raised his hand to wave back, then straightened up, saluted and disappeared. Danny Kavanagh understood completely that the sides had hardened, for Flanagan, for him.

"I'll be damned, Danny, that's just about the first time I ever saw you miss. So close, too."

"Paddy Flanagan, Joe, just couldn't do it."

Liam Lynch understood, but he was furious. "Damn it, Danny, he would've shot you if he could."

"Yes, sir, I think he would have. I'll not miss again."

Once the mines exploded in the Public Record Office section of the Four Courts and the fires spread, the end was foregone. After three days and nights of heavy shelling, the full-scale Free-State assault engulfed the Republican garrison. Some men, like Liam Lynch, managed to escape;

his hold on life temporary. Some, like Cathal Brugha, died in a heroic last stand, martyred in the Republican cause. Men like Rory O'Connor, Joe McKenna and Danny Kavanagh were captured and disarmed by a contingent under the command of Liam Tobin, the director of the Twelve Apostles in 1919. First they were herded into Mountjoy Prison. Later, Danny and Joe were transferred to Kilmainham Gaol on Dublin's Inchicore Road; the same place where, in May of 1906, Danny's father, Jimmy Kavanagh, was shot by British Army troops against a wall of the Stonebreakers Yard. Rory O'Connor stayed in "The Joy" with the most prominent organizers of the Anti-Treaty rebellion.

Danny Kavanagh said he would, but he did not shoot anyone at the Four Courts.

"What the hell's going on, Danny? What'd we do?"

"Not a clue, Joe. They're sure in a hurry though."

Armed guards, bayonets fixed, lips set flat as crimped steel, herded them at the quick step into the great hall of Kilmainham Gaol. The men on the floor stopped their restless grumbling when Sean O'Muirthile, commander of the military jail, appeared above them on the central staircase. Many prisoners could not see him because of the iron cage that surrounded it, but when he started to speak, silence fell. His words hit the stone and stopped, no echo, then fell dead to the floor below.

"Men, I have the sad duty to report that yesterday, in County Cork, our Commander-in-Chief, Michael Collins, was ambushed and killed by Irregulars. I cannot stress firmly enough that we will tolerate no demonstrations, no outbursts, from you. Our job is to keep order here, but there will be no reprisals while I am in charge. It is a sad day for Ireland and for us all. God help us."

O'Muirthile turned on his heel and stalked off the catwalk, two guards following him, rifles at the ready. Around the great hall, Free-State troops stood, waiting, unsure of the reaction from the population. There wasn't any; just a stunned silence.

Danny Kavanagh leaned against the wall, the back of his head beating a slow tattoo on the cold stone. His eyes were closed, and his fingers scrubbed his thumb. The skin of it was red, sore, abraded. Next to him, Joe McKenna regarded his scarred face and said, "Jaysus Christ, Danny, the Big Fella's gone. What's gonna happen? Maybe they'll shoot the lot of us. What'll we do?"

The pace of Danny's head smacking the wall had been increasing in tempo and force. When Joe spoke, he stopped and his eyes popped open, vague, unfocussed. Finally, he laughed, a nervous, unsettling, disembodied sound: "Do? There's nothing left. No one. We're gonna be in here a long time if Mulcahy gets his way."

Danny turned his empty gaze to the main doorway. Liam Tobin stood in it, watching him. Danny did not see him. Tobin shook his head and turned away.

10 September 1922,
Kilmainham Gaol, Dublin

My love,

I'm the proudest father that ever was. It's grand to hear that you're fine and the boy's fine and sound. Knew I could count on you, beautiful lass that you are.

And no, I wasn't ignoring anything. How could I? Try to understand. It's just that letters take a while to get here, not that the guards are hard about handing them over. Everything is so disorganized in Dublin, what with our lads derailing the trains so often. You shouldn't worry about me, even a little. Just concentrate on yourself and young Jack. I'm treated well enough, though this place can be terribly cold and damp. Thanks for the clothes and the writing paper and the biscuits and the tobacco; they're welcome indeed. I was right out of paper and haven't had a smoke in weeks. They feed us best they can.

I was really happy to hear that Jim Murtagh did the christening and your brother was godfather. With a line-up like that, the boy can't help but be strong and holy, to boot. I don't have words to say how much I missed seeing him born, christened. How much I miss you, my love. Your locket never leaves me.

We don't get a lot of information here. Newspapers are hard to come by, so it's mostly word of mouth. New men come all the time and bring news. Yesterday, it was Pedar Connor of our brigade. He's the Kilkenny man I told you about that plays the penny whistle like an angel. He's got one with him, and last night he really gave our spirits a boost with some of the old songs; some of the newer songs are really hard to listen to. Joe McKenna says he's sorry he couldn't make the christening. He's trying to get hold of some pipes. Then all we need is a drummer.

Pedar said it looks like our side is holding its own, especially in Cork and Tipperary and Kerry, even in your Mayo. I know it's hard, but we have to stick it out. We have to win, or everything we've fought for since the Rising is worthless, everything I did after was wrong, and my brother died for nothing. Rest his soul, I'm beginning to understand the Big Fella's reasons for what he did—as much as any man can. I'm just relieved it was Cork No.1 that killed him, not my boys in No. 2. With him gone, it looks like Mulcahy is in charge. That could mean anything. Like most of the men in here, I still think we can get everything we want from the English if all this would stop and we fought for a Republic on a united front. Maybe that's what Collins wanted, too. I was never sure, and now we'll never know.

Jim Murtagh told me a while ago that once the border was set in a divided Ulster it would be almost impossible to change. I don't believe it. Even Joe McKenna seems to have come round to my way of thinking. We talk about it a lot when we're let out into the Stonebreakers Yard to get a bit of exercise.

I can hear you asking. My fingers are just fine, thank you. On the other matter, I don't know what to tell you. Some of us have been released, but they signed the pledge not to bear arms against the Treaty. I can't bring myself to do that. I'm still a Captain in the IRA, not one of the "Irregulars," like we're being called. Neither can men like Joe or Pedar.

Don't fret, don't worry, I'm safe enough. The guards are Irish and civilized, after all. I even know a few of them from my Dublin days. I've never said, but Liam Tobin has a lot of authority here, sort of runs the place, day to day. He's an old IRB man, a friend of the Big Fella. I worked with him right up to when I left for Cork. He was always fair with me and stops in to have a word once in a while. When I first got here, he took the time to point out the cells that Pearse and Connolly and even your Countess Markievicz were held in after the Rising. It was a strange feeling.

I hope you are suitably impressed. This might be the longest letter I've ever written in one go. Then again, I've lots of time on my hands. I'll close now.

The light is failing from the window, and we try to use the candles as little as we can.

Say hello to Jim and Matt and Mick and Mary and every one. Kiss young Jack for me. He needs a brother.

"Till time and times are done," my love. "Till time and times are done." Believe in this: there is no chance, none, that I won't get out of here to be with you, soonest. My eyes are closed. I am touching you.

Your loving Husband,
Danny

7 December 1922,
Kilmainham Gaol, Dublin

Dear Matt,

Word didn't reach me until yesterday when new men came in. I was very sorry to hear that your Louth Brigade had to retreat from Drogheda when so many Free-Staters showed up. Seems that place is always at the center of trouble. I've never been one to interfere in your business, but I have to say that once Collins was killed and Mulcahy took over, I've been very worried about Sophie, and young Jack, and Mary, and you. From what I hear from Sophie, Jim Murtagh better keep his head down and stay out of Ulster for the time. Father Liam, I hope, has enough sense to keep his mouth shut in Belfast. Mick tells me that he's pretty well gone to ground with his people in Cullyhanna because he's getting no support at all from the south.

I can't believe they executed Erskine Childers because he had a gun that the Big Fella himself gave him. It's mad. He was a politician, not a soldier. Collins gave me the Webley I used to have, after all. Everyone here thinks it was only because Childers was Anti-Treaty and working with President de Valera to try to get it renegotiated. I'll tell you straight that a lot of the men here are more ready to fight than ever. I don't blame them one bit.

Liam Lynch seems to have gone off his nut about reprisals. The O/C of the prisoners here, Brian Sheehy, told us at the last officers' meeting that Lynch issued orders for the killing of all sorts of people in the Provisional Government. This morning, Dublin No. 1 executed two of them. Now the blood will really start.

I think it really is time for you and all to head for Mayo and Tourmakeady. Even though the rain never stops, we're strong there, and Mulcahy's people would think twice about trying anything.

We're getting on well enough here, though staying warm is a full time job. Because the weather has been so bad outside, we're not allowed into the Stonebreakers Yard for exercise. I don't mind. Walking by the wall where my father and Pearse and Connolly and the others were shot is not my idea of fun. Instead, they give us free time to mingle with the other prisoners in the main hall. It's very big, high, and there's an iron cage over the main stairway, with bars over the walkways and tiers. Still, with so many men in one room it almost gets warm. The women prisoners go to the chapel where Plunkett was married the night before the Brits shot him.

Please take care of yourself. Greetings to all from the "Republican University." That's what somebody christened this place. It's not a joke. You know what to do if I don't make it out of here.

Éirinn go Brách,
Danny

"Danny, wake up. Didn't you hear it?"

"Christ, Joe, how can a man hear anything when he's asleep in the middle of the night? What's got your wind up?"

"Somebody was at the door, doing something. Don't know what."

"Light the candle, then. We'll have a look."

The small cell was perhaps seven feet wide by ten long. The ceiling so high that the light from the smoking stub of candle did not reach it. On the wall opposite the heavy iron door, a small, barred window, high up, just visible. Joe McKenna took the wavering candle to the door, knelt and picked up a small, folded piece of paper that had been slid under it. He inspected it carefully, marveling at its whiteness in his grimy fingers, then handed it to Danny. "Addressed to you," he said, the words hanging as a stream of steam in the frigid, close air.

Danny sat on the edge of his bunk and unfolded it. He held it in his left hand, studying it; the index and middle fingers of his right began scrubbing his thumb as he read the quickly scrawled note aloud:

Kavanagh,

No need to know who I am. I know you from the old days. Two things: 1. This AM Mulcahy authorized executions in Mountjoy of 4 Courts organizers. Rory O'Connor, Liam Mellows, Joe McKelvey, Dick Barrett shot to even score for government people. 2. Got word from an Apostle that you have trouble on the way from up north—Inniskeen. Plans to get inside here shortly. Don't know how. True facts, true warning.

A Friend

Danny knew well enough that the writer, and probably the "Apostle" as well, was Liam Tobin. The two prisoners sat on the edges of their cots, heads lowered, despair, sorrow at the deaths, the waste, like a dank, cold blanket over them. The candle guttered and went out. Danny spoke first into the crystalline dark: "Mulcahy, the bastard. He told me once I had no right as a soldier to settle things with these fucking Devlins. 'No vendettas,' he said. What the hell does he call this, then? O'Connor was one bristly old cock, but he was never tried or convicted of anything. Shite. Joe McKelvey was from Belfast; I knew his family. Christ, they're all insane. Light another candle, Joe, please. Don't want any more dark just now."

"Where do you think this Devlin'll try, Danny?"

"If he's smart, could only be one place, Joe. In the big hall, when there's plenty of people about. He'll figure to get away in the confusion with the help of a guard or two. He's a dead man."

"Right you are, Danny mine, dead as a Dublin hoor."

Nothing happened for two weeks. No more notes were slipped under the thick, black iron cell door. In the aftermath of the executions at "The Joy," morale among the prisoners sank like an anchor in the stew of the Liffey. Among them were men who had had enough of killing, enough of reprisals, others who were ready to take the pledge, renounce the Republican ideal, at least for a time, so they could go home to their families. Still others, and there were many, wanted more blood. To a man, though, they agreed that this Devlin scum would have to die. Here, at least, they had some power. No one knew when he would arrive, or who would let him in. They speculated on which guards could be bought, which ones harbored the most anger about Michael Collins.

In the great hall of Kilmainham Gaol, beneath the high, broad dome of cold, milky glass reflecting yellow gas lights, the Republican prisoners gathered on a dark, chill Saturday afternoon in late December, a distant cavalry of rain thudding above them. Some walked along the walls for exercise, some sat in groups on the stone floor, playing cards spread on prison blankets, smoking their pipes, some stood chatting with their mates, some knelt with their rosaries.

Above them, on the catwalks, guards, Free-State troops in uniform, watched casually through the flat bars. Not one of them liked this duty. The men below were Irish. Many felt they weren't criminals, foes, perhaps, in the battle for a nation, but not felons. They could feel the sorrow for the executed. For many others, the killing of the Big Fella was a splinter of bone in their throats, permanently caught. Still, the atmosphere between inmates and keepers had lightened, approached the friendly, the jovial, as Christmas neared.

Even so, the guards had the keys, the weapons, the power. That line, at least, was not diminished.

Free time was over. Guards led the men of Danny's section back to their cells, two in front, one behind. Danny and Joe McKenna were the last two in line. Just after they passed the open door of an unused cell, Joe turned to talk to Danny, but he was not there. The rear guard stood in front of the closed door, a small smile on his face. Disregarding the man's rifle, Joe charged and hit him smartly on the temple. The man dropped to the stone floor and started calling for his comrades. Joe kicked his rifle away and started wrestling with him for the keys on his belt. The prisoners at the back of the line turned with a snarl and started for the cell; those at the front formed a solid wall to prevent the two guards from returning from the front.

As soon as he was pushed into the dark cell, and the door was locked, Danny was hit from behind, in the small of his back. He dropped to his knees, then a boot kicked him in the ribs. His attacker was just a dark shape in the gloom; he could hear his ragged breathing, smell the whiskey on his breath. "This is from the Devlins of Inniskeen, Kavanagh." Danny heard the familiar click of a pistol hammer being cocked. "I'll give you a minute to pray, if you want, you bastard. More than you gave my brother. We'll be taking care of all of you after this."

The roar from outside the cell was growing, hanging in the frigid gloom like another dangerous shape. The black iron door banged open, knocking the Devlin off balance, illuminating the cell with wavering yellow gas light. Joe McKenna and five prisoners crowded in and beat him to the stone with fists and boots. A hand grabbed his wrist, and the pistol fired at the ceiling, a tremendous boom in that small space. The bullet ricocheted off the stone with two, three split-second cracks, then caught one of the men in the forearm. Quickly, the assassin was disarmed.

They could hear the guards outside shouting for help. Danny looked down at the small, red-haired man on the floor. There was blood coming from his nose. "Joe, let him up. If he wants a piece of this Kavanagh, he can have one. Come on, son, we can settle this man to man. If yer beaten, give up, and ye might just get out of here alive. If ye do, tell yer family, that they ever come near me and mine, all of ye will die—all of ye."

The prisoners backed off to give the men room. They circled each other as best they could in the small space. Danny snapped into his Apostle persona: calm, deliberate, controlled, dispassionate, deadly. The men watching, even Joe McKenna, had never seen the young, green-eyed mask of death before. It frightened them to the last man.

Danny's opponent was brave enough to shoot a man in the dark. Facing one that looked like Danny Kavanagh made him wet himself.

The Devlin crouched and made for Danny's midsection with his head. Danny hit the side of his face with a fist like a block of Irish oak, and he bounced off the wall. Devlin raised his fists and waded in, knowing he had to stall long enough for help to arrive. First, Danny broke his nose, then his cheek, then his jaw. The Devlin was on his knees, dark blood spilling from his eyes, his nose, his mouth and one ear. He hadn't hit Danny Kavanagh once. From the crowd in the doorway, a man shouted: "Kill the bastard, Danny, spill his fuckin brains." Other men took it up. "Kill the bastard. Kill the bastard." It spread to a tribal chant, a ritual hymn to death, an invocation against powerlessness, defeat, despair.

Danny listened to the chanting, the dry, rusty taste of killing on his tongue. He looked down at his opponent. The man wiped his face with his sleeve and steadied himself with a fist on the stone, then pushed to stand. "Just give it up, Devlin.

Give it up. Live another day, man," Danny said, the fury subsiding at the look of such a beaten man.

The Devlin rushed again, blindly. Danny took his face in his right hand and crushed his skull on the stone wall of Kilmainham Gaol. The body dropped like a sack of damp coal. The prisoners who could see what happened roared their approval. As Danny stared at the body, the old look of sadness swept his face, quickly replaced by a new look of exhaustion, uselessness. He bent and picked up the revolver, opened the breech and emptied the shells on the ground. With it hanging from his hand, he pushed through the crowd outside. The guard's rifle was still on the floor. He took it, barrel first, and walked through the prisoners to the head of the line. They parted for him, slow eddies in a sea of thickening blood.

When he got to the front, Liam Tobin was waiting for him among the guards. The one who had pushed him into the cell had his hands high on the wall, his face against the stone. Danny handed the rifle and pistol to Tobin, and then walked toward his cell without a word. Liam Tobin stared at the prisoners for a moment, then said, "Alright, men. All over now. Back to your cells. You Irregulars will have a lapse of memory about this, and so will we. Otherwise, there will be serious repercussions. I trust I'm understood." He turned to the guard against the wall, grabbed him by the hair and pushed him toward the cell. "You, you piece of shite, go clean that up. Then get yer gear and be as far away from here as possible in ten minutes. If the commandant hears about what you did, you'll be up against the wall in the Stonebreakers right smartly."

The men were relieved, subdued, as they filed by Tobin. They all felt that for once justice had been served. Joe McKenna mumbled a "thank you" as he passed. Tobin snarled at him: "Get the fuck back inside, now."

10. "NOTHING BUT SHAME"

Two guards held Danny hard against the wall, rifle barrels across his chest; two more had Joe McKenna by the arms. Liam Tobin was in the cell, glasses perched on the end of his nose, head bowed, lips quivering, reading from a typed official document: "Joe McKenna, by order of the Provisional Government of the Irish Free State, you are to be executed forthwith for your part in the Four Courts Insurrection by Irregular Forces and for your refusal to pledge your allegiance to the duly elected Government of Ireland aforesaid."

Danny snarled, "Bullshite, Liam. That's just the feckin little fella takin revenge on Lynch, and you know it. Killin his cousin will get his attention quick enough. Put a stop to it; you've got some kind of influence with him, don't ye? There's no reason for this—none. Just more stupid waste. You can't do this. Don't. Please. For all the things we did together. Christ, man, just think of what it'll do to the rest of the men in here."

Tobin looked over Danny's shoulder as he spoke, frozen stare at stone. "Sorry, Danny, there's absolutely nothing I can do. Try to believe I've already tried. There's no way out. If I don't do it; they'll send somebody who will. It's not up to me. You can come if you think it'll help your friend. Later, we have to talk."

Joe McKenna was unable to speak as they led him into the Stonebreakers Yard and put him up against the wall where so many Irish martyrs had been christened. Danny Kavanagh stood in front of him, lighting his cigarette from cupped hands. "Do you want the priest, Joe? They'll fetch him if you want."

"Yes, I do. Be sure to write my mother. I just don't understand what this is for. Do you?" McKenna's eyes were wide, wondering, like a little boy. His face showed no fear, just surprise building to astonishment.

"Joe, I haven't understood a damned thing since I got into this place. Listen to me, my friend. I will personally make sure this debt is paid in full, no matter how long it takes or who gets in the way. I promise you that. That little bastard has a lot to answer for. Sure, I'll write your mother—and your cousin. No worries there, son." Danny took Joe McKenna's hand and held it, looking into his eyes. Joe whispered to him, "You can't be sure it was him. No, Danny, no more. Not for me." The priest arrived, and the guards herded Danny away from the Stonebreakers wall. Danny watched from the middle of the bare yard as Joe fell to his knees for his last confession; then the priest was gone, the blindfold was on, the Lee-Enfields raised. *"Erin go bragh*, you bastards," Joe McKenna shouted as the bullets were on the way toward his chest. Liam Tobin administered the *coup de grace*. The guards must have led him back to his cell, but, afterwards, Danny could not recall how he got there. Sitting next to him was his new cell mate, Pedar Connor from Kilkenny. It was December 23rd, 1922.

Later—hours, days, weeks—he did not know, didn't care, Danny Kavanagh stood in the great Kilmainham hall, leaning against the wall, the back of his head once again beating that slow tattoo on the stone. It was the same city, the same country, same sky, perhaps, but the light reluctantly leaking down from the glass dome above was nothing, absolutely nothing, like the cascade of angels wings he had seen when he met Sophia at the train station so long ago. It fell on him with the implacability of gray sleet in one dimension.

Next to him was Pedar Connor. When Pedar began to play the penny whistle, Danny's head paused. The song was familiar to all the prisoners, but the tempo was that of a dirge, not the marching song it was meant to be. Danny did not join in the singing when the some of the men took it up. Their voices were hollow; sorrow, despair smacking off stone, notes extinguished before their time:

I am a merry ploughboy, and I ploughed the fields all day,
Till a sudden thought came to my mind that I should roam away.
For I'm sick and tired of slavery since the day that I was born,
And I'm off to join the IRA, and I'm off tomorrow morn.

And we're off to Dublin in the green, in the green,
Where the helmets glisten in the sun,
Where the bayonets flash and the rifles crash
To the echo of the Thompson gun.

I'll leave aside my pick and spade, and I'll leave aside my plough,
I'll leave aside my old gray mare, for no more I'll need them now,
And I'll take my short revolver and my bandoleer of lead,

I'll do or die I can try to avenge my country's dead.

I'll leave aside my Mary, she's the girl I do adore,
And I wonder will she think of me when she hears
the rifles roar,
And when the war is over and old Ireland she is free,
I will take her to the church to wed, and a rebel's
wife she'll be.

Pedar Connor turned to Danny to encourage him in the final chorus. The whistle lowered abruptly from the lips of his open mouth. Danny's still head was leaned back on the stone; empty green eyes staring up at the dome of roof high above. The index and middle fingers of his right hand had succeeded, finally, in removing the fingerprint from his thumb. Large, black drops of blood fell from exposed ganglia to the flagged floor as steadily as sand in an hourglass.

On the other side of the hall, another, very recent song was started by Kerry men just interned that day. They managed to spit out the first two stanzas before the guards moved in and beat them to the ground:

Take it down from the mast Irish traitors,
The flag we Republicans claim,
It can never belong to Free-Staters,
You brought on it nothing but shame.

Then leave it those who are willing,
To uphold it in war and in peace,
To those who intend to continue,
Until England's cruel tyranny cease.

2 January 1923
Strabane, Co. Tyrone

My dear Danny,

The best way to put it is that Sophia is in an absolute panic about you. She tells me you haven't written in many weeks. The problem is that we can't get any information any more—about you or the other prisoners inside the Kilmainham. Please, please, write to tell her how you are. Otherwise, I seriously doubt even her father will be able to stop her from coming to Dublin. I think you'll agree that this would not be a wise course, given the current state of things in the twenty-six counties.

For my part, it's as much as I can do to help our people in the north maintain their faith—both kinds. I've heard all sorts of rumors about what the new Royal Ulster Constabulary, the Specials and the UVF are up to, but most times it's impossible to tell unless you're on the spot. The people here are frightened out of their wits, many refuse to talk to anyone, and—for now at least—the old cause is buried.

I have nothing to tell you about the Devlins. My sources of information have dried up, but I was told, by a not very reliable informant, that the lot of them have gone to ground. Speaking of rumors, I did hear third-hand that there has been some sort of trouble in the Kilmainham that might touch on them and you. Please write and tell me what has happened and that you are in good health.

Your son is growing into a strapping lad—the image of his father. Please, Danny, if you can find it in your heart to sign the pledge and get released, I think you should. As always, that's my unofficial advice. As always—like it or not—you are in my prayers.

Yours in Christ,
Jim Murtagh

10 January 1923
Inchicore Hotel, Dublin

Danny, my love,

One of the guards told me where your cell window is. He said he recognized you from the old days. Every day, between 2 and 4, I stand on the bank of the Cammock River and look up toward it and talk to you. Kind of like the heroine in *The Tale of Two Cities*. That's a joke. Don't worry, I'm not alone. Your son protects me, and so does Father Murtagh. He pleaded with me not to come, and my father was furious, but I have to be near you, pray for you, keep you safe. Father Murtagh has been trying to see General Mulcahy, but no luck there. I remembered that you mentioned Liam Tobin as a friend, so he's been trying to get to see him, too. I hope it will do some good.

Please, please, please, again and again, write and tell me you are safe. You know for a certainty how much I love you. Close your eyes. I am touching you.

Your loving Wife,
Sophia

"Danny, are you listening, man? It's me, Liam Tobin. Look at me, for Christ's sake, I'm trying to help ye, ye gobshite." Tobin sat across a table from him in a whitewashed office of the Kilmainham. In front of them was fresh tea in a large, battered Britannia metal pot, brown mugs of thick porcelain, bread and butter on a cracked white plate with a wheat sheaf pattern. Danny sat as he had since Joe McKenna was shot: speechless, staring straight ahead, the look of sadness acid etched, an oversized prisoner-made bandage covering his thumb. Pedar Connor made sure it stayed there.

Tobin reached across the table and took Danny by his good hand. "Listen now, Danny, listen best you can. I can't tell you how, but I know for sure that there's to be more executions here. They'll say the orders come from the government, but we both know what that means. He's always had it in for you, worse since the Big Fella was killed. Don't understand that part. Anyway, what I'm trying to say is that if you don't sign the pledge right smartly, I'll be leading you to the Stonebreakers before another week is out. Do you hear me, man? The paper's right there in front of you. We'll have to be quick, before the little fella finds out what we're up to. Might cost me my job—or worse. Wake up, Danny. Jaysus, what a mess the man's in."

Frustrated, Tobin stood abruptly and walked out of the office, leaving the heavy door ajar. Jim Murtagh walked in with a bright smile, hoping for a heartily irreverent greeting from the reprobate Danny Kavanagh he remembered and loved. He stopped short, completely unprepared for the empty green eyes of the man in the chair. The priest put his hand on Danny's head, blessing him, considering what to do, something near to hysteria climbing up his legs like the silent, creeping damp of the stone around him.

Sophia Kavanagh bolted past him, took one look at her husband, and went to work. First, she handed young Jack to her priest, then poured a cup of tea for her husband. Finally, she knelt before him and put her head on his lap. "'Till time and times are done,' my love, 'Till time and times are done,'" she said first to herself, then aloud to him, beseeching his face. After a few minutes, she stood, read the pledge papers and forged her husband's name with an elegant flourish, dark eyes flashing flint blue anger.

The rain swept in dense quicksilver sheets, flag after flag, over the Partry Mountains down on Tourmakeady. The February gorse, heather, rock were as bleak, lifeless, as a cold, wet winter of hate could make them. The land seemed less asleep than beaten comatose. Even so, there was just the slightest hint of spring in the Atlantic wind that never seemed to stop in the west of Ireland. It was a horrible suggestion.

Danny Kavanagh sat in a horsehair armchair in the ancestral O'Faolain house, staring out the multi-paned window of their bedroom that overlooked Lough Mask. His head beat slowly backward against a stone wall that did not exist. He focused on nothing and did not hear the hard, gusting cracks of rain on glass, soldiers at the quick step on gravel. His mind was running on the old dream, much elaborated, much longer than before. It had become a constant waking nightmare presence, not just the torturer of sleep, but the daylight demon who loosed the images. The loop always started with what he imagined his father's death was like, in the pitiless Stonebreakers he knew so well, then swept from his brother in 1916 through six years of blood and Charlie Dalton to a similar but unimagined scene starring Joe McKenna.

Downstairs, Sophia was busy at the hob, wetting their tea. Waiting around the broad deal table were Matt O'Faolain and Jim Murtagh, plus two visitors newly arrived: Mick Kavanagh down from Cullyhanna and Seamus Woods, Commander, Third Northern Division, IRA. Their talk was low, desultory, beaten flat by their understanding that the Anti-Treaty side in the civil war had no chance whatever, that Danny Kavanagh seemed silently mad. Even the roof itself seemed to leak depression over the state of the man in the armchair upstairs. Sophia was unable to find enough chores to keep her busy. Young Jack slept in his cradle near the stove, watched by the pensive, flame-haired Mary O'Faolain. She knew, now, that the workers' state she had longed for, dreamed of, desired, was only a cruel joke told by gods she did not recognize. Even her heroic Countess Markievicz was back inside the Kilmainham for her vehement and public renunciation of the Treaty. As Minister for Labour in the second *Dail* government, she said quite clearly: "...Ireland's freedom is worth blood, and worth my blood, and I will willingly give it for it, and I appeal to the men of the *Dail* to stand true." They did not, and the IRA would never recognize this second *Dail* as legitimate, fit to govern.

Jim Murtagh cleared his throat; the sound startled even him: "Mick, I hardly know what to say, to recommend. Sophia has tried everything, so has Matt, so have I, and Mary; the doctor gives us no hope. None of us can reach him. Perhaps you, the brother, can break through, but don't get your hopes up too high."

Slowly, reluctantly, apprehensively, Mick Kavanagh mounted the stairs and entered the room. He stood, silently, brooding over the scarred profile of his heroic younger brother. In Armagh, Danny had become a Republican legend. Mick considered whether the price was worth the stature. His eyes scanned the room, stopping at a mahogany chest of drawers against the whitewashed wall. On the top were Danny's two pistols in their holsters. Liam Tobin saved them when Danny was taken prisoner at the Four Courts and gave them to Sophia when they left Kilmainham Goal. Matt O'Faolain made certain they were not loaded and no ammunition was available.

Mick was unsure if it would work, unsure of the effect, but decided anything was worth a try. Surely, it could get no worse. He pulled the Webley from its holster and broke it down to make absolutely certain it was safe. The snap of spring-loaded steel when he closed it stopped the rocking of Danny's head. Mick stole silently toward him, toward the back of his chair. He stopped, cocked the pistol, pushed it against the back of Danny's neck and said, loudly, mockingly, "Finally tracked you down, Kavanagh. This is from the Devlins of Inniskeen. We've already taken care of your wife and brat."

Danny was out of the chair with a scream. He tackled his brother, pinned him, with one hand on his chest. Somehow, he had the pistol in the other. It was pointed dead center at Mick's forehead. He pulled the trigger. Nothing. Methodically, he cocked it again. Pulled the trigger. Nothing. Again and again.

"Danny, Danny, it's me, Mick. It ain't loaded." Mick knew the green-eyed mask of death, but he had never seen it so ambivalent, methodical, detached, frozen before. The muzzle of the Webley pushed hard into his forehead, marking the skin. He searched Danny's eyes, looking for his brother. Nothing. Nothing but hot red sparks of blood in the whites, opaque, impotent fury in the green. Mick did not struggle, did not attempt to take the pistol, get up, fight back. Over and over, he said, "Danny, it's me, Mick. Your brother Mick. It ain't loaded." At first loud, then lower, more calmly, falling to a whisper. Finally, "I came all the way over here from Cullyhanna to bring you a message, Danny. Jack's wife says she knows now it wasn't your fault he died at Boland's Mill. Wasn't mine, neither. Says she wishes you and Sophie all the best. Wants to see her nephew named after him."

Danny Kavanagh's eyes shifted, dull to slanting green light. He stood up, the pistol dangling at his side. He turned and faced the window. His brother stood beside him, and minute upon slow minute marched away as they watched the grey swell of Lough Mask flogged to fury by wind and rain. When the tears fell from Danny's eyes, Mick said, "Right, then, old cock. You'll be wantin yer tay. I'll send up the woman of the house."

"That was the one, Danny, I'm sure. I can tell. Felt it."

Danny Kavanagh rested his head on his wife's shoulder and wondered at the curving, swelling beauty, the heavy rise and fall, of her bare breasts. It was as if he had never seen them before, never seen the cloud shadow broken by mid-spring sun streaming through the bubbled, wavy glass of their bedroom window, never felt ecstasy, joy, peace. The newness of it all calmed him, pleased him.

"Humm, my love, not all that sure for my own self. I think we should try again right now, just to make absolutely certain, you understand. Can't be too careful."

She blushed and tried to turn her face into the pillow, but her took her cheek and prevented it, then kissed her breast quickly. She was red but smiling, forever grateful to have her man back beside her, a gnarled wreck inside, but back among the living. Her prayers had been incessant.

"Now, now, lass, it's all right. Besides, we'll have to wait a bit in any case if I'm any judge—and I think I'm the only authority in the room at present." He let go of her cheek and rested on her breast once more. "Sophie, you have to tell me now how I got out of the Kilmainham. I have no memory of it.

Not a jot." She started and stiffened; he could hear her heart gulp then speed. "Nay, lass, it's fine, God's truth. I just have to know."

"General Mulcahy wouldn't help; he even seemed hostile, angry. I remembered you wrote about Liam Tobin, so Father Murtagh and I went to see him. He didn't say very much, but it was plain he thought you were in danger unless someone got you out. He left us alone with you, and I signed your name to the pledge. Tobin had you out of that dreadful place within ten minutes. He gave me your pistols. I wanted to throw them away, but Father Murtagh wouldn't have it. He said only you could do that."

"Yes, he's a wise man, as usual. Did you hear anything at all about Pedar Connor?"

"No, not a thing. Father Murtagh wrote to Tobin, but he never got an answer. *The Irish Times* says there are still almost fifteen thousand men interned. I hope there's some sort of agreement soon so they can all go home."

"I don't see how, but we can hope for it, at least. Those lads have been through a lot and never deserved to be locked up like that—never." His voice hardened. "There's much yet to atone for, Sophie, so I'll be keeping those pistols a while. Let's never forget there are still Devlins about."

In reply, she stroked his auburn hair. He could hear the pace of her breathing shorten, the rise and fall of her breasts increasing. "Danny," she said, "Perhaps you were right."

"About what, my Mayo peach? The weather?"

She pushed him back on the mattress, her long black hair draped over his chest, her body sideways against his hip. "No, you stupid man, you know exactly what I mean."

"Oh, aye. Do me duty, is it? Don't forget now, we're after wanting a brother for young Jack. No mistake."

"Do be quiet, *Mister* Kavanagh, we have to concentrate. We'll call him Joe."

Ten o'clock on a fine late spring night, the rich, fecund smell of the lough surrounding them, the northern light a faint blue and fading, in the dooryard outside waiting, a beaded wooden bucket full of sea water and clams. Around the kitchen table sat Matt O'Faolain, Danny, Mick and Seamus Woods. Woods, a small, slight, bespectacled man who could easily have been a librarian, was the speaker. "Should have known right enough last year when I got no response atall from Dublin when I asked for help in Ulster. This letter from

Liam Lynch spells things out pretty well, boys. Outside just a few places, like Mayo here and Kerry, we're beat, plain and simple. Seems de Valera wants to come to terms with the Provisional Government. Just like him, too. Lynch is being realistic, I think, but he won't go for straight out defeat or downing of arms—just yet at least.

"Far as arms go, we're pretty thin on the ground. But I did meet with one Joe McGarrity from Philadelphia when he was over last year, just before the Free-Staters got wind of him and kicked him out of the country. McGarrity promised to help our cause with arms and money, but we should all bear in mind he was the Big Fella's man, and he and the *Clann na Gael* over there weren't all that reliable in '16. Still, we'll see what we can do on that front shortly—see if we can trust him. It's no secret he's on the outs with Dev, though. We really need one of ours over there.

"Lynch, I think, has all the men still in 'The Joy' and your 'Republican University' on his mind, Danny. They've got us over a real barrel there. Anyway, there's to be a meeting of the army commanders down in Cork in ten days time to hammer out how we'll approach Mulcahy and his lot. I'll be going, of course, and I'll come right back to report what happened, what deal we want, think we can get. Danny,

Mick, Matt, the agreement we made between us in Dundalk never to stand down—uh—still stands, if I can say that?"

The three IRA officers nodded to Woods as one.

"I'll be coming along, Seamus, my duty, I think."

"Danny, your duty is done for the time. You've given more than any ten men I know."

"That's as may be, but I'll be coming nonetheless. Liam Lynch is still my commanding officer."

"Danny, I could order you to stay here, as you know, but I won't do that. However, I'd like to remind you that you did sign the pledge. If yer caught, you'll be shot on the spot."

"They've all been trying to do that these long years, Seamus. Never got them anywhere. Besides, I've no memory of signing anything. Matt, I'll be needing some Webley and Walther shells."

"Aye, Danny. What'll you say to the bride?"

"Haven't a clue. In that direction, gettin shot might be a real danger. Mick, what of you?"

"I'll be heading for Cullyhanna tomorrow. The wife allows as how bringin a few shekels into the house might be good for the domestic economy. Just happens I found a bottle of the Irish under a hedge. We should do it some damage, gentlemen, along with the clams."

The squad of ragged Anti-Treaty, Republican troops could see the well-formed units of the Free-State forces in the valley below. Their job was to escort Liam Lynch to the meeting of all the Anti-Treaty commanders—and Eamon de Valera—to attempt some sort of compromise that would end the civil war. Problem was, getting there. Somehow, the Free-Staters seemed to anticipate their movements, their goal, as if they had an informer's guidance. The men were tired, hungry, fed up with staying outside, week after week, without dry clothes, hot food, decent shoes, ammunition. The crags and caves of County Cork's Knockmealdown Mountains had favored them during the war with the English, but the men down below had county men among them that knew the country as well as they did. The group paused to rest in a rocky hollow high above a place known locally as "the Gap."

"Danny, I suppose I should call you a true soldier, but you shouldn't have come. It's not necessary, really, not safe. It'll be over soon, and you can go home to your wife and son. If things turn out right, this will be your last job as a Captain in the IRA as we know it. In a way, I'm relieved; in a way, I'm not. There is no possible way those people down there could

have done what they did—we could have done what we did—
to each other. It's madness, and I'm just as much to blame.
Both sides seem to have lost sight of the fact that we're
fighting over whether we'll have an Irish Republic outside
Empire or a Free State within it. That's the real question, the
only question. And, for me at least, and for you I know, that
Republic includes all of Ulster, not just three of its counties."

Liam Lynch was always a tall, waspish man, but now, lack
of proper food, being on the run for months, out manned, out
gunned, had given him the wheel ground, hatchet face of a
fugitive.

"Liam, for me it's not a question of giving up and going
home. I'm just not allowed to agree to a divided country. My
father, my brother, Joe McKenna, just won't go fer it."

Danny looked sharply to his left, his attention drawn by
movement among the rocks. Silently, he signaled to his men,
and they gathered around him and the Commander-in-Chief
of the Republican forces. About 200 yards away, Free-State
troops began advancing toward them, rock to rock, heads
low. Looked like about fifteen. "Right, boys, you take the O/C
that way. I'll stay on here a bit and slow them down. We'll
form up later in Clogheen, then Mitchelstown." Danny chose
a supine position behind a low flat rock. To his right, a pile of

tilted stones, perhaps a Neolithic burial site. He looked over the iron sights of his Lee-Enfield. It was familiar feeling. He smiled. The leather sock he wore on the pad of his permanently enlarged right thumb squeaked on the stock.

The advancing troops were extremely wary, timing their moves carefully, not advancing as a unit. Danny watched for a minute or two, then began picking them off, one at a time, trying to wound, not kill. They returned fire, wildly, seemingly uncertain where he was. After he shot the third Irish soldier, the detachment began retreating. Danny smiled again, but it faded quickly when he heard a fusillade from the direction his squad had taken. He moved warily toward the sound, on his way to his men, Clogheen, Mitchelstown.

He was always one short step behind. By the time Danny got to Mitchelstown, night was falling. He slipped through the back door of the house. In the parlor, Liam Lynch lay dying, a Free-State bullet through his body, just above the hip. Danny stood quietly, still, transfixed, looking down at the gasping, bloody foam of breath slowing. He had an instant of crushing uncertainty, the terrifying Kilmainham strangulation coming over him. Lynch looked up at him. "Danny, go to Woods. He's the best one left now. And McGarrity, don't forget McGarrity in Philadelphia. He's your last hope."

Danny Kavanagh was headed for Tourmakeady, but he had one more job to do on the way. Getting a rifle in Dublin shouldn't prove all that difficult. Finding him, the strutting cock, should be easy.

He tracked him to Dublin Castle and set up his firing position on the roof of the block of buildings overlooking the Ship Street entrance. He knew well enough that General Mulcahy fancied the Turk's Head Chop House for lunch. It was just around the corner. No need to be taken by car, no need, now, for bodyguards. Strange, he thought, how all the old, hated institutions, the old haunts of the oppressor, had been occupied so quickly by the new men in power. He snorted through his nose and said to himself aloud, "Guess it ain't strange, really."

Lying on his stomach, Danny Kavanagh waited. As usual, the late spring weather in Dublin was atrocious, peals of rain falling on him as he looked down barrel of the Lee-Enfield. The downpour stopped, briefly. He knew General Mulcahy immediately; by his side Paddy Flanagan. Mulcahy held out his hand, palm up, then both men laughed and, between rain squalls, they began a leisurely stroll toward their lunch and his position. The general was speaking rapidly, drawing what looked like invisible exclamation points in the air. "Not a hard shot," Danny thought, as he removed the small piece of chamois he had used to protect the breech of his weapon from the rain. "Might even have time to get them both." He smiled as he lined up the head of General Mulcahy.

His mind ran to their first meeting, in Vaughan's Hotel. Across the table from him were Mulcahy, Michael Collins, Dick McKee. Mulcahy would be the last of the brilliant young masterminds who created a new Ireland. He started from the reverie. The general was another twenty paces closer to him. Danny lined up his head once more, an easier shot. His finger touched the trigger. He thought, quickly, of Joe McKenna up against the Stonebreakers wall, and his trigger finger tightened. Then images of his wife's white body in bed at Tourmakeady; his son in his cradle by the stove; Jim Murtagh looking at him as they spoke at the house in Newgrange.

"Alright, Joe, alright. No. I remember what you said. That's an end on it. Just more bloody waste. No vendettas," he said to himself and stood up in full view, the rifle cradled in his arms. General Mulcahy looked up and saw him, only some twenty yards away, and opened his mouth to call out.

Danny Kavanagh threw the rifle over the side to the street below, then took off his soft hat so there would be no mistake. He saluted the general, turned and walked away.

Sophia sat on a canvas deck chair on the first full day after the *Caronia* sailed from Liverpool. Her ticket certainly wasn't first class, but her father, Matt O'Faolain, came up with the money for a second class passage to New York City. "Because of the wee ones," he said. Beside her, young Jack was busy scanning the passengers walking the deck in the stiff Atlantic breeze. "Takin names," Danny had called it once. Joe, just three months old, was wrapped tightly in a shawl, nestled into her bosom. He was sleeping peacefully—for the moment. He'd wake, shortly: hungry, noisy, demanding. Of the two, she knew with a mother's certainty, Joe was most like his father. Jack was cast in her side of the family's mold: silent and patient, more interested in slow introspection and careful observation than instinct and rash action, very unlike his namesake, Danny's dead brother, in that way. The difference satisfied her immensely.

It was the best decision, the only decision, if Danny Kavanagh was to survive. From the IRA perspective, it was good strategy to have one of their own finally and firmly among the *Clann na Gael* in America, something that the Big Fella had always envisioned, ironic as that was now. Especially someone with the impeccable Republican credentials of the Twelve Apostles. His fame preceded him. It would become extremely useful in the endless struggle for a united Ireland.

A porter came with the pot of tea she had ordered, along with the biscuits she'd soften in it for Jack. Underneath her cup, a scrap of paper was scrawled with a short message. She recognized the handwriting:

> An admiring and devoted deck hand would like to meet you on the lower fantail at 10 tonight. I won't come if there's anyone nearby.

She stood there, waiting, straining to see the old world fading in the far distance. To her, the ship's wake was as the parting of the waters. Like so many fleeing Irish before her, it seemed a possible end to turmoil, sadness, grief, uncertainty, fear. She prayed, silently, for the time to come, for the new world over the horizon, for the dead she left behind, for her husband, children, family, priest. She knew too little about where she was going and what she might find there, other than the usual "streets of gold" reports in the newspapers at home. A country girl, a county girl, from a small island with a more or less homogenous population on England's always vulnerable flank, the pictures she had seen of skyscrapers, mobs of people on the streets from all over the world in New York, Philadelphia, Boston, Chicago, simply terrified her. She knew full well that all these sprawling cities had large Catholic Irish populations and she would be protected among them. That did not help her at all.

Suddenly, he was next to her. "Shush, love, let's just step over here under the stairs," he said in a whisper. They retreated to the shadows; kissed each other as if it never had happened before, held each other silently, not scared, exactly, but wondering, apprehensive. At least that was how Danny Kavanagh felt.

Finally, Danny spoke up. "Sorry again about the deck hand business, my love, but we can't be too careful. The papers I've got are good, so there's no way they can trace my name. Once we clear immigration on Ellis Island, we'll meet up in Philadelphia as arranged. You do have the addresses still, don't you, and the instructions and the money and the names and telephone numbers, train station, tickets, and...?"

Her beautiful chin almost rested on her chest; she nodded. He took her face in his hands and raised it to look in her eyes. "Sophie, I know there's a lot of uncertainty, but we've got to trust in all the preparations made for us with McGarrity and the *Clann*. The job's all set up for me, and I can finally go back to my trade. We'll be safe, at least. The house they've got for us should be fine for the time. Our first house of our own. We'll have to be wary and tread carefully. From what I've been told, there are just as many splits over there as there were at home, only no Kilmainham, no internment."

"I know, I know, Danny, but I'm just fearful that we'll be walking into the same thing, only in a different place far, far from home, without the friends, comrades we know we can trust. At least it's a comfort that all the internees have been freed, but it's not over, is it?"

"No, Sophie, it's not over, never will be while partition exists, as well you know. Ulster's six counties are the Kilmainham now, just a bigger one for people like us. I think I know what you're thinking but not saying, my wild Mayo girl."

He took off his jacket and unbuckled the leather shoulder holster holding the heavy Webley pistol that had been with him for what seemed so long. Over nearly eight years, it had gotten heavier and heavier, a blued steel tabernacle for all the dead, all the treachery, uselessness, waste, shame. These were not hosts he cared to swallow. Calmly, he walked to the rail and dropped it over the side with his healed right hand.

"What of the other one, Danny?"

"Not just yet, my love. There are still Devlins in this world. Back there, over there, even here at sea."

Neither one considered for an instant what simmering, ancient burdens, what writhing, ambivalent spirits, their souls—and the souls of their sons—carried from the old world to the new.

Made in the USA
Charleston, SC
19 January 2010